WHOLE PIECES

Edited by Alice Quine

Design by Marijka Kostiw

Cover Illustration: "Grandma's Pride" by Stephanie Nelson
Scholastic Art Awards Winner

ISBN 0-590-35579-1

12 11 10 9 8 7 6 5 4 3 2   9   2 3/9
                                                                         31

ACKNOWLEDGMENTS

Grateful acknowledgment is made to the following authors and publishers for the use of copyrighted materials. Every effort has been made to obtain permission to use previously published material. Any errors or omissions are unintentional.

Brandt & Brandt Literary Agents for "My Father Sits in the Dark" by Jerome Weidman. From MY FATHER SITS IN THE DARK AND OTHER STORIES by Jerome Weidman. Copyright 1934 and renewed 1962 by Jerome Weidman.

Don Congdon Associates, Inc. for "The Scribe" by Kristin Hunter. Copyright © 1968 by Kristin E. Lattany. From GUESTS IN THE PROMISED LAND by Kristin Hunter. Reprinted by permission of Don Congdon Associates, Inc.

Doubleday & Company, Inc. for "The Sky Is Gray" by Ernest J. Gaines. From BLOODLINES by Ernest J. Gaines. Copyright © 1963, 1964, 1968 by Ernest J. Gaines. Used by permission of Doubleday, a division of BANTAM, DOUBLEDAY, DELL PUBLISHING GROUP, INC.

Gloria Gonzalez for "The Boy With Yellow Eyes" by Gloria Gonzalez. Copyright © 1987 by Gloria Gonzalez. From VISIONS, edited by Donald R. Gallo. Copyright © 1987 by Donald R. Gallo.

Harcourt Brace Jovanovich, Inc. for "A Visit of Charity" by Eudora Welty. From A CURTAIN OF GREEN AND OTHER STORIES by Eudora Welty. Copyright 1941 and renewed 1969 by Eudora Welty. Reprinted by permission of Harcourt Brace Jovanovich, Inc.

The Jesse Stuart Foundation for "Split Cherry Tree" by Jesse Stuart. Copyright 1938 by Esquire Inc. Copyright © renewed Jesse Stuart. Reprinted by permission of The Jesse Stuart Foundation, P.O. Box #391, Ashland, KY 41114.

Random House, Inc. for "Amigo Brothers" by Piri Thomas. From STORIES FROM EL BARRIO by Piri Thomas. Copyright © 1978 by Piri Thomas. Reprinted by permission of Alfred A. Knopf, Inc. "Lost Sister" by Dorothy M. Johnson. Copyright 1951 by Dorothy M. Johnson. Reprinted from THE HANGING TREE by Dorothy M. Johnson, by permission of Ballantine Books, a division of Random House, Inc. "Neighbour Rosicky" by Willa Cather. Copyright 1932 by Willa Cather & renewed 1960 by The Executors of the Estate of Willa Cather. Reprinted from FIVE STORIES by Willa Cather, by permission of Alfred A. Knopf, Inc.

Russell & Volkening, Inc. for "The New Mirror" by Ann Petry. Copyright 1947 by Ann Petry, renewed in 1975 by Ann Petry. Originally appeared in *The New Yorker* Magazine. Reprinted by permission of Russell & Volkening as agents for the author.

Scholastic Inc. for "Ta-Na-E-Ka" by Mary Whitebird. Copyright © 1967 by Scholastic Inc. All rights reserved.

Amy Tan for "Two Kinds" by Amy Tan. Copyright © 1989 by Amy Tan. Originally appeared in *The Atlantic*.

The William Saroyan Foundation for "Where I Come From People Are Polite" by Willam Saroyan. Copyright © 1989 by The William Saroyan Foundation.

Like the patchwork quilt on the cover, *Whole Pieces* was put together by many hands. For suggesting their favorite stories, for contributing their advice, and for sharing their resources, the editor would like to thank the following people:

Marjorie Burns, Lisa Crawley, Laura Galen, Gerald Gladney, Kamau Gladney, Marijka Kostiw, Robert Quine, Kathy Robinson, Jeannette Sanderson, Laura Sherman, Lauren Weidenman.

CONTENTS

AMIGO BROTHERS

Piri Thomas

Antonio Cruz and Felix Vargas were both seventeen years old. They were so together in friendship that they felt themselves to be brothers. They had known each other since childhood, growing up on the Lower East Side of Manhattan in the same tenement building on Fifth Street between Avenue A and Avenue B.

Antonio was fair, lean, and lanky, while Felix was dark, short, and husky. Antonio's hair was always falling over his eyes, while Felix wore his black hair in a natural Afro style.

Each youngster had a dream of someday becoming lightweight champion of the world. Every chance they had the boys worked out, sometimes at the Boys Club on 10th Street and Avenue A and sometimes at the pro's gym on 14th Street. Early morning sunrises would find them running along the East River Drive, wrapped in sweat shirts, short towels around their necks, and handkerchiefs Apache style around their foreheads.

While some youngsters were into street negatives, Antonio and Felix slept, ate, rapped, and dreamt positive. Between them, they had a collection of *Fight* magazines second to none, plus a scrapbook filled with torn tickets to every boxing match they had ever attended, and some clippings of their own. If asked a question about any given fighter, they would immediately zip out from their memory banks divisions, weights, records of fights, knock-outs, technical knockouts, and draws or losses.

Each had fought many bouts representing their community and had won two gold-plated medals plus a silver and bronze medallion. The difference was in their style. Antonio's lean form and long reach made him the better boxer, while Felix's short and muscular frame made him the better slugger. Whenever they had met in the ring for sparring sessions, it had always been hot and heavy.

Now, after a series of elimination bouts, they had been informed that they were to meet each other in the division finals that were scheduled for the seventh of August, two weeks away — the winner to represent the Boys Club in the Golden Gloves Championship Tournament.

The two boys continued to run together along the East River Drive. But even when joking with each other, they both sensed a wall rising between them.

One morning less than a week before their bout, they met as usual for their daily work-out. They fooled around with a few jabs at the air, slapped skin, and then took off, running lightly along the dirty East River's edge.

Antonio glanced at Felix, who kept his eyes purposely straight ahead, pausing from time to time to do some fancy leg work while throwing one-twos followed by upper cuts to an imaginary jaw. Antonio then beat the air with a barrage of body blows and short devastating lefts with an overhand jaw-breaking right.

After a mile or so, Felix puffed and said, "Let's stop a while, bro. I think we both got something to say to each other."

Antonio nodded. It was not natural to be acting as though nothing unusual was happening when two ace-boon bud-dies were going to be blasting each other within a few short days.

They rested their elbows on the railing separating them from the river. Antonio wiped his face with his short towel. The sunrise was now creating day.

Felix leaned heavily on the river's railing and stared across to the shores of Brooklyn. Finally, he broke the silence.

"Hey, man. I don't know how to come out with it."

Antonio helped. "It's about our fight, right?"

"Yeah, right." Felix's eyes squinted at the rising orange sun.

"I've been thinking about it too. In fact, since we found out it was going to be me and you, I've been awake at night, pulling punches on you, trying not to hurt you."

"Same here. It ain't natural not to think about the fight. I mean, we both are terrific fighters and we both want to win. But only one of us can win. There ain't no draws in the eliminations."

Felix tapped Antonio gently on the shoulder. "I don't mean to sound like I'm bragging, bro. But I wanna win, fair and square."

Antonio nodded quietly, "Yeah. We both know that in the ring the better man wins. Friend or no friend, brother or no . . ."

Felix finished it for him. "Brother. Tony, let's promise something right here. Okay?"

"If it's fair, I'm for it." Antonio admired the courage of a tug boat pulling a barge five times its welterweight size.

"It's fair, Tony. When we get into the ring, it's gotta be like we never met. We gotta be like two heavy strangers that want the same thing and only one can have it. You understand, don'tcha?"

"Sí, I know." Tony smiled. "No pulling punches. We go all the way."

"Yeah, that's right. Listen, Tony. Don't you think it's a good idea if we don't see each other until the day of the fight? I'm going to stay with my Aunt Lucy in the Bronx. I can use Gleason's Gym for working out. My manager says he got some sparring partners with more or less your style."

Tony scratched his nose pensively. "Yeah, it would be better for our heads." He held out his hand, palm upward. "Deal?"

"Deal." Felix lightly slapped open skin.

"Ready for some more running?" Tony asked lamely.

"Naw, bro. Let's cut it here. You go on. I kinda like to get things together in my head."

"You ain't worried, are you?" Tony asked.

"No way, man." Felix laughed out loud. "I got too much smarts for that. I just think it's cooler if we split right here. After the fight, we can get it together again like nothing ever happened."

The *amigo* brothers were not ashamed to hug each other tightly.

"Guess you're right. Watch yourself, Felix. I hear there's some pretty heavy dudes up in the Bronx. Take it easy, okay?"

"Okay. You watch yourself too."

Tony jogged away. Felix watched his friend disappear from view, throwing rights and lefts. Both fighters had a lot of psyching up to do before the big fight.

The days in training passed much too slowly. Although they kept out of each other's way, they were aware of each other's progress via the ghetto grapevine.

The evening before the big fight, Tony made his way to the roof of his tenement. In the quiet early dark, he peered over the ledge. Six stories below the lights of the city blinked and the sounds of cars mingled with the curses and the laughter of children in the street. He tried not to think of Felix, feeling he had succeeded in psyching his mind. But only in the ring would he really know. To spare Felix hurt, he would have to knock him out, early and quick.

Up in the South Bronx, Felix decided to take in a movie in an effort to keep Antonio's face away from his fists. The flick was *The Champion* with Kirk Douglas, the third time Felix was seeing it.

When Felix finally left the theater, he had figured out how to psyche himself for tomorrow's fight. It was Felix the Champion vs. Antonio the Challenger.

He walked up some dark streets, deserted except for small

pockets of wary-looking kids wearing gang colors. Despite the fact that he was Puerto Rican like them, they eyed him as a stranger to their turf. Felix did a fast shuffle, bobbing and weaving, while letting loose a torrent of blows that would demolish whatever got in its way. It seemed to impress the brothers, who went about their own business.

Finding no takers, Felix decided to split to his aunt's. Walking the streets had not relaxed him, neither had the fight flick. All it had done was to stir him up. He let himself quietly into his Aunt Lucy's apartment and went straight to bed, falling into a fitful sleep with sounds of the gong for Round One.

Antonio was passing some heavy time on his rooftop. How would the fight tomorrow affect his relationship with Felix? After all, fighting was like any other profession. Friendship had nothing to do with it. A gnawing doubt crept in. He cut negative thinking real quick by doing some speedy fancy dance steps, bobbing and weaving like mercury. The night air was blurred with perpetual motions of left hooks and right crosses. Felix, his *amigo* brother, was not going to be Felix at all in the ring. Just an opponent with another face. Antonio went to sleep, hearing the opening bell for the first round. Like his friend in the South Bronx, he prayed for victory, via a quick clean knock-out in the first round.

Large posters plastered all over the walls of local shops announced the fight between Antonio Cruz and Felix Vargas as the main bout.

The fight had created great interest in the neighborhood. Antonio and Felix were well liked and respected. Each had his own loyal following. Betting fever was high and ranged from a bottle of Coke to cold hard cash on the line.

Antonio's fans bet with unbridled faith in his boxing skills. On the other side, Felix's admirers bet on his dynamite-packed fists.

Felix had returned to his apartment early in the morning

of August 7th and stayed there, hoping to avoid seeing
Antonio. He turned the radio to *salsa* music sounds and then
tried to read while waiting for word from his manager.

The fight was scheduled to take place in Tompkins Square
Park. It had been decided that the gymnasium of the Boys
Club was not large enough to hold all the people who were
sure to attend. In Tompkins Square Park, everyone who
wanted could view the fight, whether from ringside or
window fire escapes or tenement rooftops.

The morning of the fight Tompkins Square was a beehive
of activity with numerous workers setting up the ring, the
seats, and the guest speakers' stand. The scheduled bouts
began shortly after noon and the park had begun filling up
even earlier.

The local junior high school across from Tompkins Square
Park served as the dressing room for all the fighters. Each
was given a separate classroom with desk tops, covered with
mats, serving as resting tables. Antonio thought he caught a
glimpse of Felix waving to him from a room at the far end
of the corridor. He waved back just in case it had been him.

The fighters changed from their street clothes into fighting
gear. Antonio wore white trunks, black socks, and black
shoes. Felix wore sky blue trunks, red socks, and white
boxing shoes. Each had dressing gowns to match their
fighting trunks with their names neatly stitched on the back.

The loudspeakers blared into the open windows of the
school. There were speeches by dignitaries, community
leaders, and great boxers of yesteryear. Some were well
prepared, some improvised on the spot. They all carried
the same message of great pleasure and honor at being part
of such an historic event. This great day was in the tradition
of champions emerging from the streets of the Lower East
Side.

Interwoven with the speeches were the sounds of the other
boxing events. After the sixth bout, Felix was much relieved

when his trainer Charlie said, "Time change. Quick knock-out. This is it. We're on."

Waiting time was over. Felix was escorted from the classroom by a dozen fans in white T-shirts with the word FELIX across their fronts.

Antonio was escorted down a different stairwell and guided through a roped-off path.

As the two climbed into the ring, the crowd exploded with. a roar. Antonio and Felix both bowed gracefully and then raised their arms in acknowledgment.

Antonio tried to be cool, but even as the roar was in its first birth, he turned slowly to meet Felix's eyes looking directly into his. Felix nodded his head and Antonio responded. And both as one, just as quickly, turned away to face his own corner.

Bong — bong — bong. The roar turned to stillness.

"Ladies and Gentlemen. *Señores y Señoras.*"

The announcer spoke slowly, pleased at his bilingual efforts.

"Now the moment we have all been waiting for — the main event between two fine young Puerto Rican fighters, products of our Lower East Side. In this corner, weighing 134 pounds, Felix Vargas. And in this corner, weighing 133 pounds, Antonio Cruz. The winner will represent the Boys Club in the tournament of champions, the Golden Gloves. There will be no draw. May the best man win."

The cheering of the crowd shook the windowpanes of the old buildings surrounding Tompkins Square Park. At the center of the ring, the referee was giving instructions to the youngsters.

"Keep your punches up. No low blows. No punching on the back of the head. Keep your heads up. Understand? Let's have a clean fight. Now shake hands and come out fighting."

Both youngsters touched gloves and nodded. They turned and danced quickly to their corners. Their head towels and dressing gowns were lifted neatly from their shoulders by their trainers' nimble fingers. Antonio crossed himself. Felix did the same.

Bong! Bong! Round one. Felix and Antonio turned and faced each other squarely in a fighting pose. Felix wasted no time. He came in fast, head low, half hunched toward his right shoulder, and lashed out with a straight left. He missed a right cross as Antonio slipped the punch and countered with one-two-three lefts that snapped Felix's head back, sending a mild shock coursing through him. If Felix had any small doubt about their friendship affecting their fight, it was being neatly dispelled.

Antonio danced, a joy to behold. His left hand was like a piston pumping jabs one right after another with seeming ease. Felix bobbed and weaved and never stopped boring in. He knew that at long range he was at a disadvantage. Antonio had too much reach on him. Only by coming in close could Felix hope to achieve the dreamed-of knock-out.

Antonio knew the dynamite that was stored in his *amigo* brother's fist. He ducked a short right and missed a left hook. Felix trapped him against the ropes just long enough to pour some punishing rights and lefts to Antonio's hard midsection. Antonio slipped away from Felix, crashing two lefts to his head, which set Felix's right ear to ringing.

Bong! Both *amigos* froze a punch well on its way, sending up a roar of approval for good sportsmanship.

Felix walked briskly back to his corner. His right ear had not stopped ringing. Antonio gracefully danced his way toward his stool none the worse, except for glowing glove burns, showing angry red against the whiteness of his mid-ribs.

"Watch that right, Tony." His trainer talked into his ear. "Remember Felix always goes to the body. He'll want you to drop your hands for his overhead left or right. Got it?"

Antonio nodded, spraying water out between his teeth. He felt better as his sore midsection was being firmly rubbed.

Felix's corner was also busy.

"You gotta get in there, fella." Felix's trainer poured water over his curly Afro locks. "Get in there or he's gonna chop you up from way back."

Bong! Bong! Round two. Felix was off his stool and rushed Antonio like a bull, sending a hard right to his head. Beads of water exploded from Antonio's long hair.

Antonio, hurt, sent back a blurring barrage of lefts and rights that only meant pain to Felix, who returned with a short left to the head followed by a looping right to the body. Antonio countered with his own flurry, forcing Felix to give ground. But not for long.

Felix bobbed and weaved, bobbed and weaved, occasionally punching his two gloves together.

Antonio waited for the rush that was sure to come. Felix closed in and feinted with his left shoulder and threw his right instead. Lights suddenly exploded inside Felix's head as Antonio slipped the blow and hit him with a pistonlike left, catching him flush on the point of his chin.

Bedlam broke loose as Felix's legs momentarily buckled. He fought off a series of rights and lefts and came back with a strong right that taught Antonio respect.

Antonio danced in carefully. He knew Felix had the habit of playing possum when hurt, to sucker an opponent within reach of the powerful bombs he carried in each fist.

A right to the head slowed Antonio's pretty dancing. He answered with his own left at Felix's right eye, which began puffing up within three seconds.

Antonio, a bit too eager, moved in too close and Felix had him entangled in a rip-roaring, punching, toe-to-toe slugfest that brought the whole Tompkins Square Park screaming to its feet.

Rights to the body. Lefts to the head. Neither fighter was

giving an inch. Suddenly a short right caught Antonio
squarely on the chin. His long legs turned to jelly and his
arms flailed out desperately. Felix, grunting like a bull, threw
wild punches from every direction. Antonio, groggy, bobbed
and weaved, evading most of the blows. Suddenly his head
cleared. His left flashed out hard and straight catching Felix
on the bridge of his nose.

Felix lashed back with a haymaker right off the ghetto
streets. At the same instant, his eye caught another left hook
from Antonio. Felix swung out trying to clear the pain. Only
the frenzied screaming of those along ringside let him know
that he had dropped Antonio. Fighting off the growing haze,
Antonio struggled to his feet, got up, ducked, and threw a
smashing right that dropped Felix flat on his back.

Felix got up as fast as he could in his own corner, groggy
but still game. He didn't even hear the count. In a fog, he
heard the roaring of the crowd, who seemed to have gone
insane. His head cleared to hear the bell sound at the end of
the round. He was *mucho* glad. His trainer sat him down on
the stool.

In his corner, Antonio was doing what all fighters do when
they are hurt. They sit and smile at everyone.

The referee signaled the ring doctor to check the fighters
out. He did so and then gave his okay. The cold water
sponges brought clarity to both *amigo* brothers. They were
rubbed until their circulation ran free.

Bong! Round three — the final round. Up to now it had
been tic-tac-toe, pretty much even. But everyone knew there
could be no draw and that this round would decide the winner.

This time, to Felix's surprise, it was Antonio who came
out fast, charging across the ring. Felix braced himself but
couldn't ward off the barrage of punches. Antonio drove
Felix hard against the ropes.

The crowd ate it up. Felix tapped his gloves and commenced his attack anew. Antonio, throwing boxer's caution to the winds, jumped in to meet him.

Both pounded away. Neither gave an inch and neither fell to the canvas. Felix's left eye was tightly closed. Claret red blood poured from Antonio's nose. They fought toe-to-toe.

The sounds of their blows were loud in contrast to the silence of a crowd gone completely mute. The referee was stunned by their savagery.

Bong! Bong! Bong! The bell sounded over and over again. Felix and Antonio were past hearing. Their blows continued to pound on each other like hailstones.

Finally the referee and the two trainers pried Felix and Antonio apart. Cold water was poured over them to bring them back to their senses.

They looked around and then rushed toward each other. A cry of alarm surged through Tompkins Square Park. Was this a fight to the death instead of a boxing match?

The fear soon gave way to wave upon wave of cheering as the two *amigos* embraced.

No matter what the decision, they knew they would always be champions to each other.

Bong! Bong! Bong! "Ladies and Gentlemen. *Señores and Señoras.* The winner and representative to the Golden Gloves Tournament of Champions is . . ."

The announcer turned to point to the winner and found himself alone. Arm in arm the champions had already left the ring.

SPLIT CHERRY TREE

Jesse Stuart

"I don't mind staying after school," I says to Professor Herbert, "but I'd rather you'd whip me with a switch and let me go home early. Pa will whip me anyway for getting home two hours late."

"You are too big to whip," says Professor Herbert, "and I have to punish you for climbing up in that cherry tree. You boys knew better than that! The other five boys have paid their dollar each. You have been the only one who has not helped pay for the tree. Can't you borrow a dollar?"

"I can't," I says. "I'll have to take the punishment. I wish it would be quicker punishment. I wouldn't mind."

Professor Herbert stood and looked at me. He was a big man. He wore a gray suit of clothes. The suit matched his gray hair.

"You don't know my father," I says to Professor Herbert. "He might be called a little old-fashioned. He makes us mind him until we're twenty-one years old. He believes: 'If you spare the rod you spoil the child.' I'll never be able to make him understand about the cherry tree. I'm the first of my people to go to high school."

"You must take the punishment," says Professor Herbert. "You must stay two hours after school today and two hours after school tomorrow. I am allowing you twenty-five cents an hour. That is good money for a high school student. You can sweep the schoolhouse floor, wash the blackboards and clean windows. I'll pay the dollar for you."

I couldn't ask Professor Herbert to loan me a dollar. He never offered to loan it to me. I had to stay and help the janitor and work out my fine at a quarter an hour.

I thought as I swept the floor: "What will Pa do to me?

What lie can I tell him when I go home? Why did we ever climb that cherry tree and break it down for anyway? Why did we run crazy over the hills away from the crowd? Why did we do all of this? Six of us climbed up in a little cherry tree after one little lizard! Why did the tree split and fall with us? It should have been a stronger tree! Why did Eif Crabtree just happen to be below us plowing and catch us in his cherry tree? Why wasn't he a better man than to charge us six dollars for the tree?"

It was six o'clock when I left the schoolhouse. I had six miles to walk home. It would be after seven when I got home. I had all my work to do when I got home. It took Pa and me both to do the work. Seven cows to milk. Nineteen head of cattle to feed, four mules, twenty-five hogs. Firewood and stovewood to cut and water to draw from the well. He would be doing it when I got home. He would be mad and wondering what was keeping me!

I hurried home. I would run under the dark leafless trees. I would walk fast uphill. I would run down the hill. The ground was freezing. I had to hurry. I had to run. I reached the long ridge that led to our cow pasture. I ran along this ridge. The wind dried the sweat on my face. I ran across the pasture to the house.

I threw down my books in the chipyard. I ran to the barn to spread fodder on the ground for the cattle. I didn't take time to change my clean school clothes for my old work clothes. I ran out to the barn. I saw Pa spreading fodder on the ground for the cattle. That was my job. I ran up to the fence. I says: "Leave that for me, Pa. I'll do it. I'm just a little late."

"I see you are," says Pa. He turned and looked at me. His eyes danced fire. "What in th' world has kept you so? Why ain't you been here to help me with this work? Make a gentleman out'n one boy in th' family and this is what you get. Send you to high school and you get too ornery fer th' buzzards to smell!"

I never said anything. I didn't want to tell why I was late from school. Pa stopped scattering the bundles of fodder. He looked at me. He says: "Why are you gettin' in here this time o' night? You tell me or I'll take a hickory withe to you right here on th' spot!"

I says: "I had to stay after school." I couldn't lie to Pa. He'd go to school and find out why I had to stay. If I lied to him it would be too bad for me.

"Why did you haf to stay atter school?" says Pa.

I says: "Our biology class went on a field trip today. Six of us boys broke down a cherry tree. We had to give a dollar apiece to pay for the tree. I didn't have the dollar. Professor Herbert is making me work out my dollar. He gives me twenty-five cents an hour. I had to stay in this afternoon. I'll have to stay in tomorrow afternoon!"

"Are you telling me th' truth?" says Pa.

"I'm telling you the truth," I says. "Go and see for yourself."

"That's just what I'll do in th' mornin'," says Pa. "Jist whose cherry tree did you break down?"

"Eif Crabtree's cherry tree!"

"What was you doin' clear out in Eif Crabtree's place?" says Pa. "He lives four miles from th' County High School. Don't they teach you no books at that high school? Do they jist let you get out and gad over th' hillsides? If that's all they do, I'll keep you at home, Dave. I've got work here fer you to do!"

"Pa," I says, "spring is just getting here. We take a subject in school where we have to have bugs, snakes, flowers, lizards, frogs, and plants. It is biology. It was a pretty day today. We went out to find a few of these. Six of us boys saw a lizard at the same time sunning on a cherry tree. We all went up the tree to get it. We broke the tree down. It split at the forks. Eif Crabtree was plowing down below us. He ran up the hill and got our names. The other boys gave their dollar apiece. I didn't have mine. Professor Herbert put mine in for me. I have to work it out at school."

"Poor man's son, huh," says Pa. "I'll attend to that myself in th' mornin'. I'll take keer o' 'im. He ain't from this county nohow. I'll go down there in th' mornin' and see 'im. Lettin' you leave your books and galavant all over th' hills. What kind of a school is it nohow! Didn't do that, my son, when I's a little shaver in school. All fared alike too."

"Pa, please don't go down there," I says. "Just let me have fifty cents and pay the rest of my fine. I don't want you to go down there! I don't want you to start anything with Professor Herbert!"

"Ashamed of your old pap, are you, Dave," says Pa, "atter the way I've worked to raise you! Tryin' to send you to school so you can make a better livin' than I've made."

I thought once I'd run through the woods above the barn just as hard as I could go. I thought I'd leave high school and home forever! Pa could not catch me! I'd get away! I couldn't go back to school with him. He'd have a gun and maybe he'd shoot Professor Herbert. It was hard to tell what he would do. I could tell Pa that school had changed in the hills from the way it was when he was a boy, but he wouldn't understand. I could tell him we studied frogs, birds, snakes, lizards, flowers, insects. But Pa wouldn't understand. If I did run away from home it wouldn't matter to Pa. He would see Professor Herbert anyway. He would think that high school and Professor Herbert had run me away from home. There was no need to run away. I'd just have to stay, finish foddering the cattle, and go to school with Pa the next morning.

The moon shone bright in the cold March sky. I finished my work by moonlight. Professor Herbert really didn't know how much work I had to do at home. If he had known he would not have kept me after school. He would have loaned me a dollar to have paid my part on the cherry tree. He had never lived in the hills. He didn't know the way the hill boys had to work so that they could go to school. Now he was teaching in a County High School where all the boys who attended were from hill farms.

After I'd finished doing my work I went to the house and ate my supper. Pa and Mom had eaten. My supper was getting cold. I heard Pa and Mom talking in the front room. Pa was telling Ma about me staying in after school.

"I had to do all th' milkin' tonight, chop th' wood myself. It's too hard on me atter I've turned ground all day. I'm goin' to take a day off tomorrow and see if I can't remedy things a little. I'll go down to that high school tomorrow. I won't be a very good scholar fer Professor Herbert nohow. He won't keep me in atter school. I'll take a different kind of lesson down there and make 'im acquainted with it."

"Now, Luster," says Mom, "you jist stay away from there. Don't cause a lot o' trouble. You can be jailed fer a trick like that. You'll get th' Law atter you. You'll jist go down there and show off and plague your own boy Dave to death in front o' all th' scholars!"

"Plague or no plague," says Pa, "he don't take into consideration what all I haf to do here, does he? I'll show 'im it ain't right to keep one boy in and let the rest go scot-free. My boy is good as th' rest, ain't he? A bullet will make a hole in a schoolteacher same as it will anybody else. He can't do me that way and get by with it. I'll plug 'im first. I aim to go down there bright and early in the mornin' and get all this straight! I aim to see about bug larnin' and this runnin' all over God's creation huntin' snakes, lizards, and frogs. Ransackin' th' country and goin' through cherry orchards and breakin' th' trees down atter lizards! Old Eif Crabtree ought to a-poured th' hot lead into 'em instead o' chargin' six dollars fer th' tree! He ought to a-got old Herbert the first one!"

I ate my supper. I slipped upstairs and lit the lamp. I tried to forget the whole thing. I studied plane geometry. Then I studied my biology lesson. I could hardly study for thinking about Pa. "He'll go to school with me in the morning. He'll take a gun for Professor Herbert! What will Professor Herbert think of me! I'll tell him when Pa leaves that I couldn't help it. But Pa might shoot him. I hate to go with Pa. Maybe he'll cool off about it tonight and not go in the morning."

Pa got up at four o'clock. He built a fire in the stove. Then he built a fire in the fireplace. He got Mom up to get breakfast. Then he got me up to help feed and milk. By the time we had our work done at the barn, Mom had breakfast ready for us. We ate our breakfast. Daylight came and we could see the bare oak trees covered white with frost. The hills were white with frost.

"Now, Dave," says Pa, "let's get ready fer school. I aim to go with you this mornin' and look into bug larnin', frog larnin', lizard and snake larnin', and breakin' down cherry trees! I don't like no sicha foolish way o' larnin' myself."

Pa hadn't forgot. I'd have to take him to school with me. He would take me to school with him. I was glad we were going early. If Pa pulled a gun on Professor Herbert there wouldn't be so many of my classmates there to see him.

I knew that Pa wouldn't be at home in the high school. He wore overalls, big boots, a blue shirt and a sheepskin coat and a slouched black hat gone to seed at the top. He put his gun in its holster. We started trudging toward the high school across the hill.

It was early when we got to the County High School. Professor Herbert had just got there. I just thought as we walked up the steps into the schoolhouse: "Maybe Pa will find out Professor Herbert is a good man. He just doesn't know him. Just like I felt toward the Lambert boys across the hill. I didn't like them until I'd seen them and talked to them, then I liked them and we were friends. It's a lot in knowing the other fellow."

"You're th' Professor here, ain't you?" says Pa.

"Yes," says Professor Herbert, "and you are Dave's father?"

"Yes," says Pa, pulling out his gun and laying it on the seat in Professor Herbert's office. Professor Herbert's eyes got big behind his black-rimmed glasses when he saw Pa's gun. Color came into his pale cheeks.

"Jist a few things about this school I want to know," says Pa. "I'm tryin' to make a scholar out'n Dave. He's the only one out'n eleven youngins I've sent to high school. Here he comes in late and leaves me all th' work to do! He said you's all out bug huntin' yesterday and broke a cherry tree down. He had to stay two hours atter school yesterday and work out money to pay on that cherry tree! Is that right?"

"W-w-why," says Professor Herbert, "I guess it is."

He looked at Pa's gun.

"Well," says Pa, "this ain't no high school. It's a damn bug school, a lizard school, a snake school! It ain't no damn school nohow!"

"Why did you bring that gun?" says Professor Herbert to Pa.

"You see that little hole," says Pa as he picked up the long blue .44 and put his finger on the end of the barrel. "A bullet can come out'n that hole that will kill a schoolteacher same as it will any other man. It will kill a rich man same as a poor man. It will kill a man. But atter I come in and saw you, I know'd I wouldn't need it. This maul o'mine could do you up in a few minutes."

Pa stood there, big, hard, brown-skinned, and mighty beside of Professor Herbert. I didn't know Pa was so much bigger and harder. I'd never seen Pa in a schoolhouse before. I'd seen Professor Herbert. He always looked big before to me. He didn't look big standing beside of Pa.

"I was only doing my duty," says Professor Herbert, "Mr. Sexton, and following the course of study the state provided us with."

"Course o' study!" says Pa. "What study? Bug study? Varmint study? Takin' youngins to th' woods. Boys and girls all out there together a-galavantin' in the brush and kickin' up their heels and their poor old ma's and pa's at home a-slavin' to keep 'em in school and give 'em a education!"

Students are coming into the schoolhouse now. Professor Herbert says: "Close the door, Dave, so others won't hear."

I walked over and closed the door. I was shaking like a leaf in the wind. I thought Pa was going to hit Professor Herbert every minute. He was doing all the talking. His face was getting red. The red color was coming through the brown, weather-beaten skin on Pa's face.

"It jist don't look good to me," says Pa, "a-takin' all this whole swarm of youngins out to pillage th' whole deestrict. Breakin' down cherry trees. Keepin' boys in atter school."

"What else could I have done with Dave, Mr. Sexton?" says Professor Herbert. "The boys didn't have any business all climbing that cherry tree after one lizard. One boy could have gone up the tree and got it. The farmer charged us six dollars. It was a little steep, I think, but we had it to pay. Must I make five boys pay and let your boy off? He said he didn't have the dollar and couldn't get it. So I put it in for him. I'm letting him work it out. He's not working for me. He's working for the school!"

"I jist don't know what you could a-done with 'im," says Pa, "only a-larruped 'im with a withe! That's what he needed!"

"He's too big to whip," says Professor Herbert, pointing to me. "He's a man in size."

"He's not too big for me to whip," says Pa. "They ain't too big until they're over twenty-one! It jist didn't look fair to me! Work one and let th' rest out because they got th'

money. I don't see what bugs has got to do with a high
school! It don't look good to me nohow!"

Pa picked up his gun and put it back in its holster. The red
color left Professor Herbert's face. He talked more to Pa. Pa
softened a little. It looked funny to see Pa in the high school
building. It was the first time he'd ever been there.

"We're not only hunting snakes, toads, flowers, butterflies,
lizards," says Professor Herbert, "but, Mr. Sexton, I was
hunting dry timothy grass to put in an incubator and raise
some protozoa."

"I don't know what that is," says Pa. "Th' incubator is th'
new-fangled way o' cheatin' th' hens and raisin' chickens. I
ain't so sure about th' breed o' chickens you mentioned."

"You've heard of germs, Mr. Sexton, haven't you?" says
Professor Herbert.

"Jist call me Luster if you don't mind," says Pa, very casual
like.

"All right, Luster, you've heard of germs, haven't you?"

"Yes," says Pa, "but I don't believe in germs. I'm sixty-
five years old and I ain't seen one yet!"

"You can't see them with your naked eye," says Professor
Herbert. "Just keep that gun in the holster and stay with me
in the high school today. I have a few things I want to show
you. That scum on your teeth has germs in it."

"What," says Pa, "you mean to tell me I've got germs on
my teeth!"

"Yes," says Professor Herbert. "The same kind as we
might be able to find in a living black snake if we dissect it!"

"I don't mean to dispute your word," says Pa, "but
damned if I believe it. I don't believe I have germs on my
teeth!"

"Stay with me today and I'll show you. I want to take you
through the school anyway. School has changed a lot in the
hills since you went to school. I don't guess we had high
schools in this county when you went to school."

"No," says Pa, "jist readin', writin', and cipherin'. We didn't have all this bug larnin' and findin' germs on your teeth and in the middle o' black snakes! Th' world's changin'."

"It is," says Professor Herbert, "and we hope all for the better. Boys like your own there are going to help change it. He's your boy. He knows all of what I've told you. You stay with me today."

"I'll shore stay with you," says Pa. "I want to see th' germs off'n my teeth. I jist want to see a germ. I've never seen one in my life. Seein' is believin', Pap allus told me."

Pa walks out of the office with Professor Herbert. I just hoped Professor Herbert didn't have Pa arrested for pulling his gun. Pa's gun has always been a friend to him when he goes to settle disputes.

The bell rang. School took up. I saw the students when they marched in the schoolhouse look at Pa. They would grin and punch each other. Pa just stood and watched them pass in at the schoolhouse door. Two long lines marched in the house. The boys and girls were clean and well-dressed. Pa stood over in the schoolyard under a leafless elm, in his sheepskin coat, his big boots laced in front with buckskin and his heavy socks stuck above his boot tops. Pa's overalls' legs were baggy and wrinkled between his coat and boot tops. His blue work shirt showed at the collar. His big black hat showed his gray-streaked black hair. His face was hard and weather-tanned to the color of ripe fodder blade. His hands were big and gnarled like the roots of the elm tree he stood beside.

When I went to my first class I saw Pa and Professor Herbert going around over the schoolhouse. I was in my geometry class when Pa and Professor Herbert came in the room. We were explaining our propositions on the blackboard. Professor Herbert and Pa just quietly came in and sat down for a while. I heard Fred Wurts whisper to

Glenn Armstrong: "Who is that old man? Lord, he's a rough-looking scamp." Glenn whispered back: "I think he's Dave's pap." The students in geometry looked at Pa. They must have wondered what he was doing in school. Before the class was over, Pa and Professor Herbert got up and went out. I saw them together down on the playground. Professor Herbert was explaining to Pa. I could see the outline of Pa's gun under his coat when he'd walk around.

At noon in the high school cafeteria Pa and Professor Herbert sat together at the little table where Professor Herbert always ate by himself. They ate together. The students watched the way Pa ate. He ate with his knife instead of his fork. A lot of the students felt sorry for me after they found out he was my father. They didn't have to feel sorry for me. I wasn't ashamed of Pa after I found out he wasn't going to shoot Professor Herbert. I was glad they had made friends. I wasn't ashamed of Pa. I wouldn't be as long as he behaved.

In the afternoon when we went to biology Pa was in the class. He was sitting on one of the high stools beside the microscope. We went ahead with our work just as if Pa wasn't in the class. I saw Pa take his knife and scrape tartar from one of his teeth. Professor Herbert put it on the lens and adjusted the microscope for Pa. He adjusted it and worked awhile. Then he says: "Now, Luster, look! Put your eye right down to the light. Squint the other eye!"

Pa put his head down and did as Professor Herbert said: "I see 'em," says Pa. "Who'd a-ever thought that? Right on a body's teeth! Right in a body's mouth! You're right certain they ain't no fake to this, Professor Herbert?"

"No, Luster," says Professor Herbert. "It's there. That's the germ. Germs live in a world we cannot see with the the naked eye. We must use the microscope. There are millions of them in our bodies. Some are harmful. Others are helpful."

Pa holds his face down and looks through the microscope. We stop and watch Pa. He sits upon the tall stool. His knees are against the table. His legs are long. His coat slips up behind when he bends over. The handle of his gun shows. Professor Herbert quickly pulls his coat down.

"Oh, yes," says Pa. He gets up and pulls his coat down. Pa's face gets a little red. He knows about his gun and he knows he doesn't have any use for it in high school.

"We have a big black snake over here we caught yesterday," says Professor Herbert. "We'll chloroform him and dissect him and show you he has germs in his body too."

"Don't do it," says Pa. "I believe you. I jist don't want to see you kill the black snake. I never kill one. They are good mousers and a lot o' help to us on the farm. I like black snakes. I jist hate to see people kill 'em. I don't allow 'em killed on my place."

The students look at Pa. They seem to like him better after he said that. Pa with a gun in his pocket but a tender heart beneath his ribs for snakes, but not for man! Pa won't whip a mule at home. He won't whip his cattle.

Professor Herbert took Pa through the laboratory. He showed him the different kinds of work we were doing. He showed him our equipment. They stood and talked while we worked. Then they walked out together. They talked louder when they got out in the hall.

When our biology class was over I walked out of the room. It was our last class for the day. I would have to take my broom and sweep two hours to finish paying for the split cherry tree. I just wondered if Pa would want me to stay. He was standing in the hallway watching the students march out. He looked lost among us. He looked like a leaf turned brown on the tree among the treetops filled with growing leaves.

I got my broom and started to sweep. Professor Herbert walked up and says: "I'm going to let you do that some other time. You can go home with your father. He is waiting out there."

I laid my broom down, got my books, and went down the steps.

Pa says: "Ain't you got two hours o' sweepin' yet to do?"

I says: "Professor Herbert said I could do it some other time. He said for me to go home with you."

"No," says Pa. "You are goin' to do as he says. He's a good man. School has changed from my day and time. I'm a dead leaf, Dave. I'm behind. I don't belong here. If he'll let me I'll get a broom and we'll both sweep one hour. That pays your debt. I'll hep you pay it. I'll ast 'im and see if he won't let me hep you."

"I'm going to cancel the debt," says Professor Herbert. "I just wanted you to understand, Luster."

"I understand," says Pa, "and since I understand, he must pay his debt fer th' tree and I'm goin' to hep 'im."

"Don't do that," says Professor Herbert. "It's all on me."

"We don't do things like that," says Pa; "we're just and honest people. We don't want somethin' fer nothin'. Professor Herbert, you're wrong now and I'm right. You'll haf to listen to me. I've larned a lot from you. My boy must go on. Th' world has left me. It changed while I've raised my family and plowed th' hills. I'm a just and honest man. I don't skip debts. I ain't larned 'em to do that. I ain't got much larnin' myself but I do know right from wrong atter I see through a thing."

Professor Herbert went home. Pa and I stayed and swept one hour. It looked funny to see Pa use a broom. He never used one at home. Mom used the broom. Pa used the plow. Pa did hard work. Pa says: "I can't sweep. Durned if I can. Look at th' streaks o' dirt I leave on th' floor! Seems like no work a-tall fer me. Brooms is too light 'r somethin'. I'll jist do th' best I can, Dave. I've been wrong about th' school."

I says: "Did you know Professor Herbert can get a warrant

out for you for bringing your pistol to school and showing
it in his office! They can railroad you for that!"

"That's all made right," says Pa. "I've made that right.
Professor Herbert ain't goin' to take it to court. He likes me.
I like 'im. We jist had to get together. He had the remedies.
He showed me. You must go on to school. I am as strong a
man as ever come out'n th' hills fer my years and th' hard
work I've done. But I'm behind, Dave. I'm a little man. Your
hands will be softer than mine. Your clothes will be better.
You'll allus look cleaner than your old pap. Jist remember,
Dave, to pay your debts and be honest. Jist be kind to animals
and don't bother th' snakes. That's all I got agin th' school.
Puttin' black snakes to sleep and cuttin' 'em open."

It was late when we got home. Stars were in the sky. The
moon was up. The ground was frozen. Pa took his time going
home. I couldn't run like I did the night before. It was ten
o'clock before we got the work finished, our suppers eaten.
Pa sat before the fire and told Mom he was going to take her
and show her a germ some time. Mom hadn't seen one either.
Pa told her about the high school and the fine man Professor
Herbert was. He told Mom about the strange school across
the hill and how different it was from the school in their day
and time.

TA-NA-E-KA

Mary Whitebird

My birthday drew close, and I had awful nightmares about it. I was reaching the age at which all Kaw Indians had to participate in Ta-Na-E-Ka.

Well, not all Kaws. Many of the younger families were beginning to give up the old customs.

But my grandfather, Amos Deer Leg, was devoted to tradition. He still wore beaded moccasins instead of shoes. He still kept his gray hair in tight braids.

He could speak English, but he spoke it only with white men. With his family, he used a Sioux dialect.

Grandfather was one of the last living Indians who fought against the U.S. Cavalry. He was wounded in a battle at Rose Creek. At the time, my grandfather was only eleven years old.

Eleven was a magic word among the Kaws. It was the time of Ta-Na-E-Ka, the "flowering of adulthood." It was the age when a boy could prove himself to be a warrior, and a girl took the first steps to womanhood.

"I don't want to be a warrior," my cousin, Roger Deer Leg, told me. "I'm going to become an accountant."

"None of the other tribes make girls go through the endurance ritual," I told my mother.

"It won't be as bad as you think, Mary," my mother said. "Once you've gone through it, you'll never forget it. You'll be proud."

I even complained to my teacher, Mrs. Richardson. I felt that a white woman would side with me.

She didn't. "All of us have rituals of one kind or another," Mrs. Richardson said. "Besides, how many girls get to compete equally with boys? Don't look down on your heritage."

Heritage, indeed! I would not live on a reservation for the rest of my life. I was a good student. I loved school. My fantasies were about knights in armor. I didn't think that being an Indian was very exciting.

But I've always thought that the Kaw started the women's liberation movement. No other Indian tribe treated women more "equally" than the Kaw.

The Kaw allowed men and women to eat together. A Kaw woman always had the right to refuse a future husband. This was true even if her father had arranged the marriage.

The wisest old women often sat in tribal councils. Plus, most Kaw legends revolve around "Good Woman." She was a kind of super-squaw. Good Woman helped Kaw warriors win battle after battle.

And girls as well as boys had to go through Ta-Na-E-Ka.

The ceremony was different from tribe to tribe. But Ta-Na-E-Ka was a test of survival.

"Endurance is the highest quality of the Indian," my grandfather said. "To survive, we must endure. When I was a boy, Ta-Na-E-Ka was more than it is now.

"We were painted white with the juice of a sacred herb. We were sent naked into the wilderness without a knife. We couldn't return until the white had worn off. It took almost 18 days.

"We trapped food, and we ate insects and roots and berries. We watched out for enemies. Our enemies were the white soldiers and the Omaha warriors.

"These warriors were always trying to capture Kaw boys and girls during the endurance test. It was an exciting time," Grandfather said.

"What happened if you couldn't make it?" Roger asked. He was born only three days after I was. We were being trained for Ta-Na-E-Ka together. I was happy to know he was frightened, too.

"Many didn't return," Grandfather said. "Only the strongest and smartest. Mothers were not allowed to weep over those who didn't return."

"How stupid," Roger whispered. "I'd give anything to get out of it."

"What choice do we have?" I asked.

Roger gave my arm a squeeze. "Well, it's only five days."

Five days! Maybe it was better than being sent out naked for 18 days. But not much better.

We were to be sent, barefoot and in bathing suits, into the woods. Our parents put their foot down when Grandfather suggested we go naked.

For five days, we'd have to live off the land. It was May. But the days were chilly on the northern banks of the Missouri River. The nights were freezing cold.

Grandfather was in charge of the month's training for Ta-Na-E-Ka. One day he caught a grasshopper. He showed us how to pull its legs and wings off. Then we were supposed to swallow it.

I felt sick, and Roger turned green. "It's a darn good thing it's 1947," I told Roger. "You'd make a terrible warrior."

I knew one thing. This Kaw Indian girl wasn't going to swallow a grasshopper. And then I had an idea. Why hadn't I thought of it before? It would have saved nights of bad dreams about squooshy grasshoppers.

I headed straight for my teacher's house. "Mrs. Richardson," I said, "would you lend me $5?"

"What for?" she asked.

"You remember the ceremony I talked about?"

"Ta-Na-E-Ka? Of course. Your parents asked me to excuse you from school for it."

"I need some things for the ceremony," I said. "I don't want to ask my parents for the money."

"It's not a crime to borrow money, Mary. But how can you pay it back?"

"I'll baby-sit for you 10 times."

"That's more than fair." She handed me a new $5 bill. I'd never had that much money at once.

A few days later, the ritual began with a long speech from my grandfather. All our friends and relatives made jokes about their own Ta-Na-E-Ka experiences.

They told us to have a large dinner. For the next five days, we'd be eating crickets. But Roger and I weren't very hungry.

"I'll laugh about this when I'm an accountant," Roger said, trembling.

"Are you trembling?" I asked.

"What do you think?"

"I'm happy to know boys tremble, too," I said.

At six the next morning, we set off for the woods.

"Which side do you want?" Roger asked.

Roger and I were supposed to stake out separate territories. We weren't allowed to talk to each other.

"I'll go toward the river. That okay with you?" I asked.

"Sure," Roger said. "What difference does it make?"

To me, it made a lot of difference. There was a small harbor a few miles up the river. There were boats there. At least, I hoped so. I'd rather sleep in a boat than under a pile of leaves.

"Why do you keep holding your head?" Roger asked.

"Oh, nothing. Just nervous," I told him. I was afraid I'd lose the $5 bill. I had tucked it into my hair with a bobby pin.

As we came to a fork in the trail, Roger shook my hand. "Good luck, Mary."

"N'ko-n'ta," I said. It was the Kaw word for courage.

The sun was shining, and it was warm. But my bare feet began to hurt.

I saw one of the berry bushes Grandfather had told us about. The berries were orange and fat. I popped one into my mouth.

Argh! I spat it out. It was awful and bitter. Even grasshoppers were probably better tasting.

I sat down to rest my feet. A rabbit hopped out from under the berry bush. He looked at me, twitching his nose. I watched a woodpecker bore into an elm tree.

All of a sudden, I realized I was no longer frightened. Ta-Na-E-Ka might be more fun than I had thought. I got up and headed toward the harbor.

"Not one boat," I said to myself.

But the restaurant on the shore was open. I walked in, feeling silly in my bathing suit.

The man at the counter was big and tough-looking. He had only three fingers on one of his hands. He asked me what I wanted.

"A hamburger and a milk shake," I said.

"That's a pretty big breakfast," he said.

"That's what I always have for breakfast," I lied.

"Forty-five cents," he said, bringing me the food. (Back in 1947, hamburgers were 25 cents, and milk shakes were 20 cents.)

"Delicious," I thought. "Better than grasshoppers. Grandfather didn't say I couldn't eat hamburgers."

While I was eating, I had a great idea. Why not sleep in the restaurant? I went to the ladies' room and made sure the window was unlocked. Then I went back outside and played along the riverbank.

The restaurant closed at sunset. I watched the three-fingered man drive away. Then I climbed in the unlocked window. There was a night-light on, so I didn't turn on any lights.

But there was a radio on the counter. I turned it on to a music program. It was warm in the restaurant, and I was hungry. I helped myself to a glass of milk and a piece of pie.

I planned to leave money for what I'd eaten. I also planned to get up early and sneak out the window.

I turned off the radio and wrapped myself in the man's apron. The floor was hard, but I soon fell asleep.

"What the heck are you doing here, kid?"

It was the man's voice.

It was morning. I'd overslept. I was scared.

"Hold it, kid. I just wanna know what you're doing here. You lost? You must be from the reservation. Your folks must be worried sick about you. Do they have a phone?"

"Yes, yes," I answered. "But don't call them." I was shivering.

The man — Ernie — made me a cup of hot chocolate. I explained about Ta-Na-E-Ka.

"Darnedest thing I ever heard," Ernie said. "Pretty silly thing to do to a kid."

That was just what I'd been thinking for months. But when Ernie said it, I became angry.

"No, it isn't silly. It's a custom of the Kaw. We've been doing this for hundreds of years," I said. "It's why the Kaw are great warriors."

"Okay, great warrior," Ernie laughed. "Suit yourself. And if you want to stick around, it's okay with me." Ernie went to the broom closet and tossed me a bundle.

"That's the lost-and-found closet," he said. "Stuff people left on boats. Maybe there's something to keep you warm."

The sweater fitted loosely, but it felt good. I felt good. I'd found a new friend. Most important, I was surviving Ta-Na-E-Ka.

My grandfather had said that the experience would be filled with adventure. I was having my fill. Grandfather had never said we couldn't accept hospitality.

I stayed at the restaurant for the whole five days. In the mornings, I went into the woods and watched the animals. I picked flowers for each of the tables in Ernie's.

I had never felt better. I was up early enough to watch

the sun rise on the river. I went to bed after it set. I ate everything I wanted. I insisted Ernie take all my money for the
food.

I was sorry when the five days were over. I'd enjoyed every
minute with Ernie. He taught me how to make western
omelets and chili.

I told him all about the legends of the Kaw. I hadn't
realized I knew so much about my people.

Ta-Na-E-Ka was over. I came home at about 9:30 in the
evening. I was nervous all over again. What if Grandfather
asked me about the berries and the grasshoppers?

My feet were hardly cut. I hadn't lost a pound, and my
hair was combed.

"They'll be so happy to see me," I told myself. "They
won't ask too many questions."

I opened the door. My grandfather was in the front room.
He was wearing the ceremonial shirt which had belonged to
his grandfather. "N'g'da'ma," he said. "Welcome back."

I embraced my parents warmly. I let go only when I saw
my cousin Roger. He was lying on the couch. His eyes were
red and swollen.

He'd lost weight. His feet were a mass of blood and
blisters. He was moaning, "I made it, see? I made it. I'm a
warrior. A warrior."

My grandfather looked at me strangely. I was clean, well-
fed, and healthy. My parents got the message. My uncle and
aunt looked at me angrily.

Finally, my grandfather spoke. "What did you eat to keep
you so well?"

I sucked in my breath and told the truth: "Hamburgers
and milk shakes," I said.

"Hamburgers!" my grandfather growled.

"Milk shakes!" Roger moaned.

"You didn't say we *had* to eat grasshoppers," I said.

"Tell us all about your Ta-Na-E-Ka," my grandfather commanded.

I told them everything.

"That's not what I trained you for," my grandfather said sadly.

I stood up. "Grandfather, I learned that Ta-Na-E-Ka is important. I didn't think so during training. I was scared stiff of it. I handled it in my way. And I learned I had nothing to be afraid of. There's no reason in 1947 to eat grasshoppers when you can eat a hamburger."

I was shocked at my own nerve. But I liked it. "Grandfather, I'll bet you never ate one of those rotten berries yourself."

Grandfather laughed! He laughed aloud! My mother and father and aunt and uncle couldn't believe it. Grandfather never laughed. Never.

"Those berries — they are terrible," Grandfather said. "I could never swallow them. I found a dead deer on the first day of my Ta-Na-E-Ka. He kept my belly full for the whole time!"

Grandfather stopped laughing. "We should send you out again," he said.

I looked at Roger. "You're pretty smart, Mary," Roger groaned. "I'd never have thought of what you did."

"Accountants just have to be good at arithmetic," I said. "I'm terrible at arithmetic."

Roger tried to smile, but couldn't. My grandfather called me to him.

"You should have done what Roger did," he said. "But I think you realize what is happening to our people today. I think you would have passed the test at any time. You know how to exist in a world that wasn't made for Indians. I don't think you're going to have any trouble surviving."

Grandfather wasn't entirely right. But I'll tell about that another time.

THE BOY WITH YELLOW EYES

Gloria Gonzalez

Only a handful of the residents of Preston Heights recall the actual events. And even then, years and conflicting accounts have clouded the facts.

Still, in some quarters, and especially during the relentless winters unique to the hillside village, the incident is spoken of with pride and awe.

Till today, if you get a couple of old-timers in the same room, a heated debate will erupt over the mundane detail of whether Norman was ten or going on thirteen. They'll also argue whether he lost one shoe or both in the scuffle.

What the parties do agree on is that it happened in Preston Heights and it involved Norman and his next-door neighbor Willie, whose age for some reason is never questioned — thirteen.

And of course . . . the stranger.

Opinions are equally divided on whether the stranger's limp was caused by a deformed right or left leg. But everyone, to a man, can tell you exactly what the Vice President of the United States was wearing when he arrived and what he ordered for lunch. (In fact, his discarded gingham cloth napkin, since laundered, is part of the local exhibit, which includes his signature in the hotel's register.)

The only other point of total agreement is that Norman was the least likely of heroes. He had none of the qualities that could have foretold his sudden fame.

Norman was not the kind of kid who would cause you to break out in a grin if you saw him ride your way on a bike.

1. He couldn't ride a bike.
2. He rarely emerged from his house.
3. He was considered . . . well . . . weird.

This last opinion was based on the fact that Norman would only be seen heading toward or leaving the library, and always hugging an armful of books. To the townfolk it seemed unhealthy for a young boy to read so much. They predicted a total loss of eyesight by the time he reached nineteen.

Willie, however, was a kid who, had there been a Normal Kid Pageant, would have won first and tied for second and third. A dynamic baseball player, daring bike rider, crackerjack newspaper delivery boy — he was the town's delight. Never mind that he was flunking all school subjects and had a reputation as a bully, he was, after all, "a real boy."

The differences did not escape the boys themselves. Though neighbors, separated only by splintery bushes, they never as much as shared a "Hi."

To Willie, Norman was simply the kid with the yellow eyes. Not that they were actually yellow — more of a brown-hazel — but often, the way the sunlight bounced off the thick eyeglasses, it seemed to create a yellow haze.

(Years later, in a rare interview, Norman was asked if he had missed having friends while growing up. He replied: "Not at all. I had Huck and Tom Sawyer.")

To Norman, Willie was exhausting. He talked fast, ran fast, walked fast, and, he suspected, even slept fast. (If such a thing could be measured.) It was tiring just to sit behind him in class and listen to his endless chatter.

If Norman was slow motion, Willie was definitely fast forward. Which brings us to the stranger, who fit somewhere in between.

Some say the stranger arrived one early summer day on foot. Others believe he came on the bus from Boulder.

One fact is undisputed: he took a room on the second floor of McCory's hotel. Not that he had much of a choice; it was the only lodging in town. The hotel dated back to the construction of the first railroad. It had been hastily thrown together to house the army of laborers that would lay the train tracks. Unfortunately, the hilly terrain stymied the work force and the project was eventually abandoned, leaving behind three passenger and two freight cars.

George McCory, the town's undertaker, purchased the hotel and soon found he could make more money by housing the living.

The hotel parlor soon became the common milling ground. Here you could always get into a game of checkers, buy stamps, mail a letter, or receive news of neighboring towns via the traveling salesmen.

That's why when the stranger first arrived, his presence went almost unnoticed. It was only after he was still visible over a period of weeks that others became aware of him. A tall, muscular man in his thirties with a ready smile, he made a favorable impression. Maybe it was the limp. Many attributed it to the war then raging in Europe. Too polite to inquire, the hotel regulars silently accepted his "wound."

Since the man was never seen during the day and rarely till after supper, his comings and goings drew much speculation. Local gossip had it that he was an artist who'd come to Preston Heights to paint the unusual terrain. This theory was fueled by the sight of the man always carrying a dark satchel. Some held that the man was famous.

Perhaps that legend would have endured except for three insignificant, unrelated events:

1. The library decided to paint its reading room.
2. Willie's baseball coach had a tooth pulled.
3. The stranger overslept.

On the day of the "incident," Norman headed, as usual, to the library. Mrs. Brenner, the librarian, met him at the entrance and explained that due to the cleanup work the library was temporarily closed.

The thought of studying in his stuffy bedroom (no air could circulate because of all the books he ordered from Chicago and New York publishers) sent him instead to the railroad yards.

The discarded railroad cars — which had been painted a zippy burgundy when new — now bore the scars of merciless winters and oppressive summers. Vandalism and neglect had added to the toll. For too many years, kids had deemed it their own amusement park. In recent time, the decaying cars had even been abandoned by the vandals. Rumor had it that rats and raccoons openly roamed the burgundy cars.

Norman knew it wasn't true. At least once a month, when the weather was nice, he would head for the rail yard, lugging his books, to settle comfortably in a cushioned seat in car #7215, his head pressed against the wooden window frame (now paneless). When the day's shadow hit the bottom of the page, he knew to close the book and head home.

On this day, the high position of the sun assured him of at least four uninterrupted hours of reading.

Across town, in the school yard, Willie stood with friends swinging his baseball bat at air. He looked forward to practice almost as much as to the games. That's why when the coach appeared to say he had to cancel due to an impacted tooth, the teenager found himself at a loss as to what to do.

It was too early to start his newspaper money collection. Knowing it was best to strike when families were seated for dinner, he wandered aimlessly toward the rail yards with a mind to picking up some chunky rocks and using them as balls to swat about the empty field.

And so it was that he found himself in the proximity of car #7215.

The unusually warm weather had its effect on the stranger who now dozed in the freight car, an iron link away from #7215. The heat had caused him to discard his usual caution in return for a slight breeze. He had lifted the huge steel doors that slid upward, affording him a welcome breeze from the quiet countryside. The cool air had lulled his senses, stretching his customary nap long past its normal half hour.

Perhaps it was his two months of success, his feeling of invincibility, or his unconscious desire for danger that caused him to be careless this day. In any event, when he awoke, he did not bother to lower the steel door.

He opened his black satchel and removed the network of tubes, cylinders, wires, bolts, and antennas which he expertly positioned in a matter of minutes. It was by now an automatic labor. His mind refreshed by sleep, he thought ahead to the coming week when he would be safely aboard the steamer that would carry him across the ocean. The lightness of his touch, as he twisted the spidery wires, reflected his carefree attitude.

Norman's first reaction was to ignore Willie's sudden entrance.

"You see my ball go by here?"

Norman didn't even look up from the book he was reading. "No."

"Not exactly a ball, more like a rock," Willie said, sitting on the armrest of a seat, with his legs blocking the aisle.

"No," Norman answered.

Normally, Willie would have stalked out, but it was cooler inside the car, and most appealing of all, Norman looked so relaxed and comfortable that he felt compelled to ruin it.

"What are you doing, anyway?"

"Reading."

"I figured that. That's all you ever do. Aren't you afraid you're going to lose your eyesight?"

Norman's lack of response did not still Willie.

"I think reading is dumb."

"I think hitting a rock with a stick is dumb."

"Oh, yeah? You ever try it?"

"No. You ever try reading?"

"When the teacher makes me. I'd rather hit a rock. It's fun."

"So is reading."

Willie didn't buy it. "When I hit a ball, I'm *doing* something. Reading is not doing."

Norman removed his glasses and closely regarded Willie with his full attention.

"Do you know what I was *doing* when you barged in here? I was running through a haunted castle being chased by a vampire who was very, very thirsty. If that isn't 'doing,' I don't know what is."

This led to Norman's explaining the plot of Bram Stoker's *Dracula*. Willie, totally engrossed, sat on the floor listening to the tale of horror.

Norman was telling him about Renfield — and his daily diet of spiders and insects — when a distant clicking sound averted his attention.

"Probably a woodpecker," Willie said, urging the other boy to get back to the story.

Norman stretched his neck closer to the sound.

"If it is, it's the smartest woodpecker in history," Norman said, straining to hear.

Something in Norman's expression caused Willie to whisper, "What are you talking about?"

Norman swiftly signaled him to be quiet and silently crept toward the source of the tapping.

Willie, suddenly frightened for reasons he could not explain, followed closely. "What is it?" he asked, gripping his baseball bat.

The tapping was louder now.

"It's coming from the freight car." Norman dropped to the floor, his body hunched against the steel door separating them from the other car. Willie fell alongside him. "What is it?" he half pleaded.

Norman took a pencil from his pocket and began scribbling furiously on the margins of the library book. Willie noticed that he wrote with the rhythm of the clicking sound. Whenever the tapping stopped for a moment, so did Norman's pencil.

Willie glanced at the jottings, but it was difficult to make out the words. He did make out one short phrase. "End is near."

Norman and the clicking stopped at the same time.

"What does it mean?" Willie whispered, his fear growing. He had known fear once before, when a stray dog, foaming at the mouth, had cornered him behind the general store. But this was worse. Here the threat was unknown.

Norman quickly stashed the book under a seat and jumped to his feet. "We have to stop him!" he told Willie.

"Who?"

"The spy," Norman said as he slid open the heavy door and dashed outside.

A startled Willie sat frozen.

The bright sun slammed Norman in the face as he jumped from the train car and rolled underneath the freight compartment. He was silently happy to see Willie join him seconds later.

"What are we doing?" Willie asked, frightened of the answer.

"Waiting."

"For what?" he whispered.

"Him," Norman said, pointing to the underbelly of the rusted car.

Before Willie could reply, the stranger jumped from above their heads, clutching his dark suitcase. They watched as his limping form started to move away.

Norman sprung from under the car, raced after the man, and — to Willie's horror — tackled him from behind. The satchel went flying in the surprise attack.

"Grab it! Grab it!" Norman screamed.

The stranger clawed the ground and struggled to his feet, fighting like a wild man. His eyes were ablaze with hate. His arms, hands, and feet spun like a deranged windmill. His actions were swift but Norman was quicker. Try as he might to grab the boy, the man kept slashing at the air. He managed to clutch the boy's foot, but Norman quickly wiggled out of his shoe. The man grabbed him by his pants leg and pulled him to the ground.

"Do something!" Norman screamed at Willie, who stood paralyzed with fear. The man was now crouched over the boy's body and was gripping his neck.

Willie, seeing Norman's legs thrash helplessly in the air, swung his baseball bat with all his strength and caught the stranger — low and inside.

"About time," Norman coughed, massaging his throbbing neck.

Hours later, sitting in the hotel lobby with the chief of police, the boys watched wearily as swarms of people dashed up and down the stairs. They knew the man's room was being torn apart.

In the hotel kitchen the stranger was surrounded by FBI agents who had been summoned from the state capital, seventy-eight miles away. More were en route from Washington, D.C.

By nightfall the hotel was completely isolated from the public and everyone heard of how Willie and Norman had caught themselves a real-life Nazi spy.

It took weeks for the full story to emerge, and even then the citizens felt that the whole story would never be revealed. (Norman's *Dracula* book, for instance, had been whisked away by agents.) What was learned was that the man had been transmitting information to a colleague in Boulder. That man had managed to slip away and was now believed to be back in Berlin. Two of the strangers' conspirators in New

York — one a woman — were arrested and being held in a federal prison outside of Virginia.

Three months later, in a highly publicized visit, the Vice President of the United States came to Preston Heights to thank the boys personally. Film crews shot footage of the unlikely trio that would be shown in movie theaters throughout the country; Preston Heights would never be the same.

The cameras were there when Norman was asked how he had been able to understand the Morse code. "I learned it from a book," he said.

Asked how he had been able to overpower the man, Willie grinned. "Easy. I'm batting .409 on the school team."

Preston Heights blossomed under the glare of national attention. Tourists visiting the state made it a point to spend the night at McCory's hotel and gawk at the corner table in the dining room where the Vice President ate lunch with the boys and their parents.

Willie did not go on to become a major league slugger. Instead, he left Preston Heights to join the navy and rose to the rank of chief petty officer upon retirement.

Norman attended Georgetown University and went on to serve as press secretary for a New Jersey senator.

Every Christmas they exchange cards and a list of books each has read during the previous year.

Norman is still ahead of Willie, two to one.

THE SCRIBE

Kristin Hunter

We been living in the apartment over the Silver Dollar
Check Cashing Service five years. But I never had any reason
to go in there till two days ago, when Mom had to go to the
Wash-a-Mat and asked me to get some change.

And man! Are those people who come in there in some
bad shape.

Old man Silver and old man Dollar, who own the place,
have signs tacked up everywhere:

NO LOUNGING, NO LOITERING

THIS IS NOT A WAITING ROOM

and

MINIMUM CHECK CASHING FEE, 50¢

and

LETTERS ADDRESSED, 50¢

and

LETTERS READ, 75¢

and

LETTERS WRITTEN, ONE DOLLAR

And everybody who comes in there to cash a check gets
their picture taken like they're some kind of criminal.

After I got my change, I stood around for a while digging
the action. First comes an old lady with some kind of long
form to fill out. The mean old man behind the counter points
to the "One Dollar" sign. She nods. So he starts to fill it out
for her.

"Name?"

"Muskogee Marie Lawson."

"SPELL it!" he hollers.

"M, m, u, s — well, I don't exactly know, sir."

"I'll put down 'Marie,' then. Age?"

"Sixty-three my last birthday."

"Date of birth?"

"March twenty-third" — a pause — "I think, 1900."

"Look, Marie," he says, which makes me mad, hearing him first-name a dignified old gray-haired lady like that, "if you'd been born in 1900, you'd be seventy-two. Either I put that down, or I put 1910."

"Whatever you think best, sir," she says timidly.

He sighs, rolls his eyes to the ceiling, and bangs his fist on the form angrily. Then he fills out the rest.

"One dollar," he says when he's finished. She pays like she's grateful to him for taking the trouble.

Next is a man with a cane, a veteran who has to let the government know he moved. He wants old man Silver to do this for him, but he doesn't want him to know he can't do it himself.

"My eyes are kind of bad, sir, will you fill this thing out for me? Tell them I moved from 121 South 15th Street to 203 North Decatur Street."

Old man Silver doesn't blink an eye. Just fills out the form, and charges the crippled man a dollar.

And it goes on like that. People who can't read or write or count their change. People who don't know how to pay their gas bills, don't know how to fill out forms, don't know how to address envelopes. And old man Silver and old man Dollar cleaning up on all of them. It's pitiful. It's disgusting. Makes me so mad I want to yell.

And I do, but mostly at Mom. "Mom, did you know there are hundreds of people in this city who can't read and write?"

Mom isn't upset. She's a wise woman. "Of course, James," she says. "A lot of the older people around here haven't had your advantages. They came from down South, and they had to quit school very young to go to work.

"In the old days, nobody cared whether our people got an education. They were only interested in getting the crops in." She sighed. "Sometimes I think they *still* don't care. If we hadn't gotten you into that good school, you might not be able to read so well either. A lot of boys and girls your age can't, you know."

"But that's awful!" I say. "How do they expect us to make it in a big city? You can't even cross the streets if you can't read the WALK and DON'T WALK signs."

"It's hard," Mom says, "but the important thing to remember is it's no disgrace. There was a time in history when nobody could read or write except a special class of people."

And Mom takes down her Bible. She has three Bible study certificates and is always giving me lessons from Bible history. I don't exactly go for all the stuff she believes in, but sometimes it *is* interesting.

"In ancient times," she says, "no one could read or write except a special class of people known as *scribes*. It was their job to write down the laws given by the rabbis and the judges. No one else could do it.

"Jesus criticized the scribes," she goes on, "because they were so proud of themselves. But he needed them to write down his teachings."

"Man," I said when she finished, "that's something."

My mind was working double-time. I'm the best reader and writer in our class. Also it was summertime. I had nothing much to do except go to the park or hang around the library and read till my eyeballs were ready to fall out, and I was tired of doing both.

So the next morning, after my parents went to work, I took Mom's card table and a folding chair down to the sidewalk. I lettered a sign with a Magic Marker, and I was in business. My sign said:

PUBLIC SCRIBE— ALL SERVICES FREE

I set my table up in front of the Silver Dollar and waited for business. Only one thing bothered me. If the people couldn't read, how would they know what I was there for?

But five minutes had hardly passed when an old lady stopped and asked me to read her grandson's letter. She explained that she had just broken her glasses. I knew she was fibbing, but I kept quiet.

I read the grandson's letter. It said he was having a fine time in California, but was a little short. He would send her some money as soon as he made another payday. I handed the letter back to her.

"Thank you, son," she said, and gave me a quarter.

I handed that back to her too.

The word got around. By noontime I had a whole crowd of customers around my table. I was kept busy writing letters, addressing envelopes, filling out forms, and explaining official-looking letters that scared people half to death.

I didn't blame them. The language in some of those letters — "Establish whether your disability is one-fourth, one-third, one-half, or total, and substantiate in paragraph 3(b) below" — would upset anybody. I mean, why can't the government write English like everybody else?

Most of my customers were old, but there were a few young ones too. Like the girl who had gotten a letter about her baby from the Health Service and didn't know what "immunization" meant.

At noontime one old lady brought me some iced tea and a peach, and another gave me some fried chicken wings. I was really having a good time, when the shade of all the people standing around me suddenly vanished. The sun hit me like a ton of hot bricks.

Only one long shadow fell across my table. The shadow of a tall, heavy, blue-eyed cop. In our neighborhood, when they see a cop, people scatter. That was why the back of my neck was burning.

"What are you trying to do here, sonny?" the cop asks.

"Help people out," I tell him calmly, though my knees are knocking together under the table.

"Well, you know," he says, "Mr. Silver and Mr. Dollar have been in business a long time on this corner. They are very respected men in this neighborhood. Are you trying to run them out of business?"

"I'm not charging anybody," I pointed out.

"That," the cop says, "is exactly what they don't like. Mr. Silver says he is glad to have some help with the letter-writing. Mr. Dollar says it's only a nuisance to them anyway and takes up too much time. But if you don't charge for your services, it's unfair competition."

Well, why not? I thought. After all, I could use a little profit.

"All right," I tell him. "I'll charge a quarter."

"Then it is my duty to warn you," the cop says, "that it's against the law to conduct a business without a license. The first time you accept a fee, I'll close you up and run you off this corner."

He really had me there. What did I know about licenses? I'm only thirteen, after all. Suddenly I didn't feel like the big black businessman anymore. I felt like a little kid who wanted to holler for his mother. But she was at work, and so was Daddy.

"I'll leave," I said, and did, with all the cool I could muster. But inside I was burning up, and not from the sun.

One little old lady hollered, "You big bully!" and shook her umbrella at the cop. But the rest of those people were so beaten-down they didn't say anything. Just shuffled back on inside to give Mr. Silver and Mr. Dollar their hard-earned money like they always did.

I was so mad I didn't know what to do with myself that afternoon. I couldn't watch TV. It was all soap operas anyway, and they seemed dumber than ever. The library didn't appeal to me either. It's not air-conditioned, and the day was hot and muggy.

Finally I went to the park and threw stones at the swans in the lake. I was careful not to hit them, but they made good targets because they were so fat and white. Then after a while the sun got lower. I kind of cooled off and came to my senses. They were just big, dumb, beautiful birds, and not my enemies. I threw them some crumbs from my sandwich and went home.

"Daddy," I asked that night, "how come you and Mom never cash checks downstairs in the Silver Dollar?"

"Because," he said, "we have an account at the bank, where they cash our checks free."

"Well, why doesn't everybody do that?" I wanted to know.

"Because some people want all their money right away," he said. "The bank insists that you leave them a minimum balance."

"How much?" I asked him.

"Only five dollars."

"But that five dollars still belongs to you after you leave it there?"

"Sure," he says. "And if it's in a savings account, it earns interest."

"So why can't people see they lose money when they *pay* to have their checks cashed?"

"A lot of *our* people," Mom said, "are scared of banks, period. Some of them remember the Depression, when all the banks closed and the people couldn't get their money out. And others think banks are only for white people. They think they'll be insulted, or maybe even arrested, if they go in there."

Wow. The more I learned, the more pitiful it was. "Are there any black people working at our bank?"

"There didn't used to be," Mom said, "but now they have Mr. Lovejoy and Mrs. Adams. You know Mrs. Adams, she's nice. She has a daughter your age."

"I Immm," I said, and shut up before my folks started to wonder why I was asking all those questions.

The next morning, when the Silver Dollar opened, I was right there. I hung around near the door, pretending to read a copy of *Jet* magazine.

"Psst," I said to each person who came in. "I know where you can cash checks *free*."

It wasn't easy convincing them. A man with a wine bottle in a paper bag blinked his red eyes at me like he didn't believe he had heard right. A carpenter with tools hanging all around his belt said he was on his lunch hour and didn't have time. And a big fat lady with two shopping bags pushed past me and almost knocked me down, she was in such a hurry to give Mr. Silver and Mr. Dollar her money.

But finally I had a little group who were interested. It wasn't much. Just three people. Two men — one young, one old — and the little old lady who'd asked me to read her the letter from California. Seemed the grandson had made his payday and sent her a money order.

"How far is this place?" asked the young man.

"Not far. Just six blocks," I told him.

"Aw shoot. I ain't walking all that way just to save fifty cents."

So then I only had two. I was careful not to tell them where we were going. When we finally got to the Establishment Trust National Bank, I said, "This is the place."

"I ain't goin' in there," said the old man. "No sir. Not me. You ain't gettin' me in *there*." And he walked away quickly, going back in the direction we had come.

To tell the truth, the bank did look kind of scary. It was a big building with tall white marble pillars. A lot of Brink's armored trucks and Cadillacs were parked out front. Uniformed guards walked back and forth inside with guns. It might as well have had a "Colored Keep Out" sign.

Whereas the Silver Dollar is small and dark and funky and dirty. It has trash on the floors and tape across the broken windows. People going in there feel right at home.

I looked at the little old lady. She smiled back bravely.

"Well, we've come this far, son," she said. "Let's not turn back now."

So I took her inside. Fortunately Mrs. Adams' window was near the front.

"Hi, James," she said.

"I've brought you a customer," I told her.

Mrs. Adams took the old lady to a desk to fill out some forms. They were gone a long time, but finally they came back.

"Now, when you have more business with the bank, Mrs. Franklin, just bring it to me," Mrs. Adams said.

"I'll do that," the old lady said. She held out her shiny new bankbook. "Son, do me a favor and read that to me."

"Mrs. Minnie Franklin," I read aloud. "July 9, 1972. Thirty-seven dollars."

"That sounds real nice," Mrs. Franklin said. "I guess now I have a bankbook, I'll have to get me some glasses."

Mrs. Adams winked at me over the old lady's head, and I winked back.

"Do you want me to walk you home?" I asked Mrs. Franklin.

"No thank you, son," she said. "I can cross streets by myself all right. I know red from green."

And then she winked at both of us, letting us know she knew what was happening.

"Son," she went on, "don't ever be afraid to try a thing just because you've never done it before. I took a bus up here from Alabama by myself forty-four years ago. I ain't thought once about going back. But I've stayed too long in one neighborhood since I've been in this city. Now I think I'll go out and take a look at *this* part of town."

Then she was gone. But she had really started me thinking. If an old lady like that wasn't afraid to go in a bank and open an account for the first time in her life, why should *I* be afraid to go up to City Hall and apply for a license? Wonder how much they charge you to be a scribe?

MY FATHER SITS IN THE DARK

Jerome Weidman

My father has a peculiar habit. He is fond of sitting in the dark, alone. Sometimes I come home very late. The house is dark. I let myself in quietly because I do not want to disturb my mother. She is a light sleeper. I tiptoe into my room and undress in the dark. I go to the kitchen for a drink of water. My bare feet make no noise. I step into the room and almost trip over my father. He is sitting in a kitchen chair, in his pajamas, smoking his pipe.

"Hello, Pop," I say.

"Hello, son."

"Why don't you go to bed, Pa?"

"I will," he says.

But he remains there. Long after I am asleep I feel sure that he is still sitting there, smoking.

Many times I am reading in my room. I hear my mother get the house ready for the night. I hear my kid brother go to bed. I hear my sister come in. I hear her do things with jars and combs until she, too, is quiet. I know she has gone to sleep. In a little while I hear my mother say good night to my father. I continue to read. Soon I become thirsty. (I drink a lot of water.) I go to the kitchen for a drink. Again I almost stumble across my father. Many times it startles me. I forget about him. And there he is — smoking, sitting, thinking.

"Why don't you go to bed, Pop?"

"I will, son."

But he doesn't. He just sits there and smokes and thinks. It worries me. I can't understand it. What can he be thinking about? Once I asked him.

"What are you thinking about, Pa?"

"Nothing," he said.

Once I left him there and went to bed. I awoke several hours later. I was thirsty. I went to the kitchen. There he was. His pipe was out. But he sat there, staring into a corner of the kitchen. After a moment I became accustomed to the darkness. I took my drink. He still sat and stared. His eyes did not blink. I thought he was not even aware of me. I was afraid.

"Why don't you go to bed, Pop?"

"I will, son," he said. "Don't wait up for me."

"But," I said, "you've been sitting here for hours. What's wrong? What are you thinking about?"

"Nothing, son," he said. "Nothing. It's just restful. That's all."

The way he said it was convincing. He did not seem worried. His voice was even and pleasant. It always is. But I could not understand it. How could it be restful to sit alone in an uncomfortable chair far into the night, in darkness?

What can it be?

I review all the possibilities. It can't be money. I know that. We haven't much, but when he is worried about money he makes no secret of it. It can't be his health. He is not reticent about that either. It can't be the health of anyone in the family. We are a bit short on money, but we are long on health. (Knock wood, my mother would say.) What can it be? I am afraid I do not know. But that does not stop me from worrying.

Maybe he is thinking of his brothers in the old country. Or of his mother and two step-mothers. Or of his father. But they are all dead. And he would not brood about them like that. I say brood, but it is not really true. He does not brood. He does not even seem to be thinking. He looks too peaceful, too, well not contented, just too peaceful, to be brooding. Perhaps it is as he says. Perhaps it is restful. But it does not seem possible. It worries me.

If I only knew what he thinks about. If I only knew that

he thinks at all. I might not be able to help him. He might
not even need help. It may be as he says. It may be restful.
But at least I would not worry about it.

Why does he just sit there, in the dark? Is his mind failing?
No, it can't be. He is only fifty-three. And he is just as keen-
witted as ever. In fact, he is the same in every respect. He
still likes beet soup. He still reads the second section of the
Times first. He still wears wing collars. He still believes that
Debs could have saved the country and that T.R. was a tool
of the moneyed interests. He is the same in every way. He
does not even look older than he did five years ago. Everybody remarks about that. Well-preserved, they say. But he
sits in the dark, alone, smoking, staring straight ahead of
him, unblinking, into the small hours of the night.

If it is as he says, if it is restful, I will let it go at that. But
suppose it is not. Suppose it is something I cannot fathom.
Perhaps he needs help. Why doesn't he speak? Why doesn't
he frown or laugh or cry? Why doesn't he do something?
Why does he just sit there?

Finally I become angry. Maybe it is just my unsatisfied
curiosity. Maybe I *am* a bit worried. Anyway, I become
angry.

"Is something wrong, Pop?"

"Nothing, son. Nothing at all."

But this time I am determined not to be put off. I am angry.

"Then why do you sit here all alone, thinking, till late?"

"It's restful, son. I like it."

I am getting nowhere. Tomorrow he will be sitting there
again. I will be puzzled. I will be worried. I will not stop
now. I am angry.

"Well, what do you *think* about, Pa? Why do you just sit
here? What's worrying you? What do you think about?"

"Nothing's worrying me, son. I'm all right. It's just restful.
That's all. Go to bed, son."

My anger has left me. But the feeling of worry is still there.

I must get an answer. It seems so silly. Why doesn't he tell me? I have a funny feeling that unless I get an answer I will go crazy. I am insistent.

"But what do you *think* about, Pa? What is it?"

"Nothing, son. Just things in general. Nothing special. Just things."

I can get no answer.

It is very late. The street is quiet and the house is dark. I climb the steps softly, skipping the ones that creak. I let myself in with my key and tiptoe into my room. I remove my clothes and remember that I am thirsty. In my bare feet I walk to the kitchen. Before I reach it I know he is there.

I can see the deeper darkness of his hunched shape. He is sitting in the same chair, his elbows on his knees, his cold pipe in his teeth, his unblinking eyes staring straight ahead. He does not seem to know I am there. He did not hear me come in. I stand quietly in the doorway and watch him.

Everything is quiet, but the night is full of little sounds. As I stand there motionless I begin to notice them. The ticking of the alarm clock on the icebox. The low hum of an automobile passing many blocks away. The swish of papers moved along the street by the breeze. A whispering rise and fall of sound, like low breathing. It is strangely pleasant.

The dryness in my throat reminds me. I step briskly into the kitchen.

"Hello, Pop," I say.

"Hello, son," he says. His voice is low and dream-like. He does not change his position or shift his gaze.

I cannot find the faucet. The dim shadow of light that comes through the window from the street lamp only makes the room seem darker. I reach for the short chain in the center of the room. I snap on the light.

He straightens up with a jerk, as though he has been struck. "What's the matter, Pop?" I ask.

"Nothing," he says. "I don't like the light."

"What's the matter with the light?" I say. "What's wrong?"

"Nothing," he says. "I don't like the light."

I snap the light off. I drink my water slowly. I must take it easy, I say to myself. I must get to the bottom of this.

"Why don't you go to bed? Why do you sit here so late in the dark?"

"It's nice," he says. "I can't get used to lights. We didn't have lights when I was a boy in Europe."

My heart skips a beat and I catch my breath happily. I begin to think I understand. I remember the stories of his boyhood in Austria. I see the wide-beamed *kretchma*, with my grandfather behind the bar. It is late, the customers are gone, and he is dozing. I see the bed of glowing coals, the last of the roaring fire. The room is already dark, and growing darker. I see a small boy, crouched on a pile of twigs at one side of the huge fireplace, his starry gaze fixed on the dull remains of the dead flames. The boy is my father.

I remember the pleasure of those few moments while I stood quietly in the doorway watching him.

"You mean there's nothing wrong? You just sit in the dark because you like it, Pop?" I find it hard to keep my voice from rising in a happy shout.

"Sure," he says. "I can't think with the light on."

I set my glass down and turn to go back to my room. "Good night, Pop," I say.

"Good night," he says.

Then I remember. I turn back. "What do you think about, Pop?" I ask.

His voice seems to come from far away. It is quiet and even again. "Nothing," he says softly. "Nothing special."

TWO KINDS

Amy Tan

My mother believed you could be anything you wanted to be in America. You could open a restaurant. You could work for the government and get good retirement. You could buy a house with almost no money down. You could become rich. You could become instantly famous.

"Of course, you can be prodigy, too," my mother told me when I was nine. "You can be best anything. What does Auntie Lindo know? Her daughter, she is only best tricky."

America was where all my mother's hopes lay. She had come to San Francisco in 1949 after losing everything in China: her mother and father, her family home, her first husband, and two daughters, twin baby girls. But she never looked back with regret. Things could get better in so many ways.

We didn't immediately pick the right kind of prodigy. At first my mother thought I could be a Chinese Shirley Temple. We'd watch Shirley's old movies on TV as though they were training films. My mother would poke my arm and say, "*Ni kan*. You watch." And I would see Shirley tapping her feet, or singing a sailor song, or pursing her lips into a very round O while saying "Oh, my goodness."

"*Ni kan*," my mother said, as Shirley's eyes flooded with tears. "You already know how. Don't need talent for crying!"

Soon after my mother got this idea about Shirley Temple, she took me to the beauty training school in the Mission District and put me in the hands of a student who could barely hold the scissors without shaking. Instead of getting big fat curls, I emerged with an uneven mass of crinkly black fuzz. My mother dragged me off to the bathroom and tried to wet down my hair.

"You look like Negro Chinese," she lamented, as if I had done this on purpose.

The instructor of the beauty training school had to lop off these soggy clumps to make my hair even again. "Peter Pan is very popular these days," the instructor assured my mother. I now had hair the length of a boy's, with curly bangs that hung at a slant two inches above my eyebrows. I liked the haircut, and it made me actually look forward to my future fame.

In fact, in the beginning I was just as excited as my mother, maybe even more so. I pictured this prodigy part of me as many different images, and I tried each one on for size. I was a dainty ballerina girl standing by the curtain, waiting to hear the music that would send me floating on my tiptoes. I was like the Christ child lifted out of the straw manger, crying with holy indignity. I was Cinderella stepping from her pumpkin carriage with sparkly cartoon music filling the air.

In all of my imaginings I was filled with a sense that I would soon become perfect. My mother and father would adore me. I would be beyond reproach. I would never feel the need to sulk, or to clamor for anything.

But sometimes the prodigy in me became impatient. "If you don't hurry up and get me out of here, I'm disappearing for good," it warned. "And then you'll always be nothing."

Every night after dinner my mother and I would sit at the Formica-topped kitchen table. She would present new tests, taking her examples from stories of amazing children that she had read in *Ripley's Believe It or Not* or *Good House-keeping, Reader's Digest*, or any of a dozen other magazines she kept in a pile in our bathroom. My mother got these magazines from people whose houses she cleaned. And since she cleaned many houses each week, we had a great assortment. She would look through them all, searching for stories about remarkable children.

The first night she brought out a story about a three-year-old boy who knew the capitals of all the states and even of most of the European countries. A teacher was quoted as saying that the little boy could also pronounce the names of the foreign cities correctly. "What's the capital of Finland?" my mother asked me, looking at the story.

All I knew was the capital of California, because Sacramento was the name of the street we lived on in Chinatown. "Nairobi!" I guessed, saying the most foreign word I could think of. She checked to see if that might be one way to pronounce *Helsinki* before showing me the answer.

The tests got harder — multiplying numbers in my head, finding the queen of hearts in a deck of cards, trying to stand on my head without using my hands, predicting the daily temperatures in Los Angeles, New York, and London. One night I had to look at a page from the Bible for three minutes and then report everything I could remember. "Now Jehoshaphat had riches and honor in abundance and . . . that's all I remember, Ma," I said.

And after seeing, once again, my mother's disappointed face, something inside me began to die. I hated the tests, the raised hopes and failed expectations. Before going to bed that night I looked in the mirror above the bathroom sink, and when I saw only my face staring back — and understood that it would always be this ordinary face — I began to cry. Such a sad, ugly girl! I made high-pitched noises like a crazed animal, trying to scratch out the face in the mirror.

And then I saw what seemed to be the prodigy side of me — a face I had never seen before. I looked at my reflection, blinking so that I could see more clearly. The girl staring back at me was angry, powerful. She and I were the same. I had new thoughts, willful thoughts — or, rather, thoughts filled with lots of won'ts. I won't let her change me, I promised myself. I won't be what I'm not.

So now when my mother presented her tests, I performed listlessly, my head propped on one arm. I pretended to be bored. And I was. I got so bored that I started counting the bellows of the foghorns out on the bay while my mother drilled me in other areas. The sound was comforting and reminded me of the cow jumping over the moon. And the next day I played a game with myself, seeing if my mother would give up on me before eight bellows. After a while I usually counted only one bellow, maybe two at most. At last she was beginning to give up hope.

Two or three months went by without any mention of my being a prodigy. And then one day my mother was watching the *Ed Sullivan Show* on TV. The TV was old and the sound kept shorting out. Every time my mother got halfway up from the sofa to adjust the set, the sound would come back on and Sullivan would be talking. As soon as she sat down, Sullivan would go silent again. She got up — the TV broke into loud piano music. She sat down — silence. Up and down, back and forth, quiet and loud. It was like a stiff, embraceless dance between her and the TV set. Finally, she stood by the set with her hand on the sound dial.

She seemed entranced by the music, a frenzied little piano piece with a mesmerizing quality, which alternated between quick, playful passages and teasing, lilting ones.

"*Ni kan*," my mother said, calling me over with hurried hand gestures. "Look here."

I could see why my mother was fascinated by the music. It was being pounded out by a little Chinese girl, about nine years old, with a Peter Pan haircut. The girl had the sauciness of a Shirley Temple. She was proudly modest, like a proper Chinese child. And she also did a fancy sweep of a curtsy, so that the fluffy skirt of her white dress cascaded to the floor like the petals of a large carnation.

In spite of these warning signs, I wasn't worried. Our family had no piano and we couldn't afford to buy one, let alone reams of sheet music and piano lessons. So I could be generous in my comments when my mother bad-mouthed the little girl on TV.

"Play note right, but doesn't sound good!" my mother complained. "No singing sound."

"What are you picking on her for?" I said carelessly. "She's pretty good. Maybe she's not the best, but she's trying hard." I knew almost immediately that I would be sorry I had said that.

"Just like you," she said. "Not the best. Because you not trying." She gave a little huff as she let go of the sound dial and sat down on the sofa.

The little Chinese girl sat down also, to play an encore of "Anitra's Tanz," by Grieg. I remember the song, because later on I had to learn how to play it.

Three days after watching the *Ed Sullivan Show* my mother told me what my schedule would be for piano lessons and piano practice. She had talked to Mr. Chong, who lived on the first floor of our apartment building. Mr. Chong was a retired piano teacher, and my mother had traded housecleaning services for weekly lessons and a piano for me to practice on every day, two hours a day, from four until six.

When my mother told me this, I felt as though I had been sent to hell. I whined, and then kicked my foot a little when I couldn't stand it anymore.

"Why don't you like me the way I am?" I cried. "I'm *not* a genius! I can't play the piano. And even if I could, I wouldn't go on TV if you paid me a million dollars!"

My mother slapped me. "Who ask you to be genius?" she shouted. "Only ask you be your best. For you sake. You think I want you to be genius? Hnnh! What for! Who ask you!"

"So ungrateful," I heard her mutter in Chinese. "If she had as much talent as she has temper, she'd be famous now."

Mr. Chong, whom I secretly nicknamed Old Chong, was very strange, always tapping his fingers to the silent music of an invisible orchestra. He looked ancient in my eyes. He had lost most of the hair on the top of his head, and he wore thick glasses and had eyes that always looked tired. But he must have been younger than I thought, since he lived with his mother and was not yet married.

I met Old Lady Chong once, and that was enough. She had a peculiar smell, like a baby that had done something in its pants, and her fingers felt like a dead person's, like an old peach I once found in the back of the refrigerator; its skin just slid off the flesh when I picked it up.

I soon found out why Old Chong had retired from teaching piano. He was deaf. "Like Beethoven!" he shouted to me. "We're both listening only in our head!" And he would start to conduct his frantic silent sonatas.

Our lessons went like this. He would open the book and point to different things, explaining their purpose: "Key! Treble! Bass! No sharps or flats! So this is C major! Listen now and play after me!"

And then he would play the C scale a few times, a simple chord, and then, as if inspired by an old unreachable itch, he would gradually add more notes and running trills and a pounding bass until the music was really something quite grand.

I would play after him, the simple scale, the simple chord, and then just play some nonsense that sounded like a cat running up and down on top of garbage cans. Old Chong would smile and applaud and say, "Very good! But now you must learn to keep time!"

So that's how I discovered that Old Chong's eyes were too

slow to keep up with the wrong notes I was playing. He went through the motions in half time. To help me keep rhythm, he stood behind me and pushed down on my right shoulder for every beat. He balanced pennies on top of my wrists so that I would keep them still as I slowly played scales and arpeggios. He had me curve my hand around an apple and keep that shape when playing chords. He marched stiffly to show me how to make each finger dance up and down, staccato, like an obedient little soldier.

He taught me all these things, and that was how I also learned I could be lazy and get away with mistakes, lots of mistakes. If I hit the wrong notes because I hadn't practiced enough, I never corrected myself. I just kept playing in rhythm. And Old Chong kept conducting his own private reverie.

So maybe I never really gave myself a fair chance. I did pick up the basics pretty quickly, and I might have become a good pianist at that young age. But I was so determined not to try, not to be anybody different, that I learned to play only the most ear-splitting preludes, the most discordant hymns.

Over the next year I practiced like this, dutifully in my own way. And then one day I heard my mother and her friend Lindo Jong both talking in a loud, bragging tone of voice so that others could hear. It was after church, and I was leaning against a brick wall, wearing a dress with stiff white petticoats. Auntie Lindo's daughter, Waverly, who was my age, was standing farther down the wall, about five feet away. We had grown up together and shared all the closeness of two sisters, squabbling over crayons and dolls. In other words, for the most part, we hated each other. I thought she was snotty. Waverly Jong had gained a certain amount of fame as "Chinatown's Littlest Chinese Chess Champion."

"She bring home too many trophy," Auntie Lindo lamented that Sunday. "All day she play chess. All day I have no time do nothing but dust off her winnings." She threw a scolding look at Waverly, who pretended not to see her.

"You lucky you don't have this problem," Auntie Lindo said with a sigh to my mother.

And my mother squared her shoulders and bragged: "Our problem worser than yours. If we ask Jing-mei wash dish, she hear nothing but music. It's like you can't stop this natural talent."

And right then I was determined to put a stop to her foolish pride.

A few weeks later Old Chong and my mother conspired to have me play in a talent show that was to be held in the church hall. By then my parents had saved up enough to buy me a secondhand piano, a black Wurlitzer spinet with a scarred bench. It was the showpiece of our living room.

For the talent show I was to play a piece called "Pleading Child," from Schumann's *Scenes From Childhood*. It was a simple, moody piece that sounded more difficult than it was. I was supposed to memorize the whole thing. But I dawdled over it, playing a few bars and then cheating, looking up to see what notes followed. I never really listened to what I was playing. I daydreamed about being somewhere else, about being someone else.

The part I liked to practice best was the fancy curtsy: right foot out, touch the rose on the carpet with a pointed foot, sweep to the side, bend left leg, look up, and smile.

My parents invited all the couples from their social club to witness my debut. Auntie Lindo and Uncle Tin were there. Waverly and her two older brothers had also come. The first two rows were filled with children either younger or older than I was. The littlest ones got to go first. They recited simple nursery rhymes, squawked out tunes on miniature violins, and twirled hula hoops in pink ballet tutus, and when they bowed or curtsied, the audience would sigh in unison,

"*Awww,*" and then clap enthusiastically.

When my turn came, I was very confident. I remember my childish excitement. It was as if I knew, without a doubt, that the prodigy side of me really did exist. I had no fear whatsoever, no nervousness. I remember thinking, This is it! This is it! I looked out over the audience, at my mother's blank face, my father's yawn, Auntie Lindo's stiff-lipped smile, Waverly's sulky expression. I had on a white dress, layered with sheets of lace, and a pink bow in my Peter Pan haircut. As I sat down, I envisioned people jumping to their feet and Ed Sullivan rushing up to introduce me to everyone on TV.

And I started to play. Everything was so beautiful. I was so caught up in how lovely I looked that I wasn't worried about how I would sound. So I was surprised when I hit the first wrong note. And then I hit another, and another. A chill started at the top of my head and began to trickle down. Yet I couldn't stop playing, as though my hands were bewitched. I kept thinking my fingers would adjust themselves back, like a train switching to the right track. I played this strange jumble through to the end, the sour notes staying with me all the way.

When I stood up, I discovered my legs were shaking. Maybe I had just been nervous, and the audience, like Old Chong, had seen me go through the right motions and had not heard anything wrong at all. I swept my right foot out, went down on my knee, looked up, and smiled. The room was quiet, except for Old Chong, who was beaming and shouting, "Bravo! Bravo! Well done!" But then I saw my mother's face, her stricken face. The audience clapped weakly, and as I walked back to my chair, with my whole face quivering as I tried not to cry, I heard a little boy whisper loudly to his mother, "That was awful," and the mother whispered back, "Well, she certainly tried."

And now I realized how many people were in the audi-

ence — the whole world, it seemed. I was aware of eyes
burning into my back. I felt the shame of my mother and
father as they sat stiffly through the rest of the show.
We could have escaped during intermission. Pride and
some strange sense of honor must have anchored my parents
to their chairs. And so we watched it all: The eighteen-year-
old boy with a fake moustache who did a magic show and
juggled flaming hoops while riding a unicycle. The breasted
girl with white makeup who sang an aria from *Madame
Butterfly* and got an honorable mention. And the eleven-year-
old boy who won first prize playing a tricky violin song that
sounded like a busy bee.

After the show the Hsus, the Jongs, and the St. Clairs,
from the Joy Luck Club, came up to my mother and father.

"Lots of talented kids," Auntie Lindo said vaguely, smiling
broadly.

"That was somethin' else," my father said, and I wondered
if he was referring to me in a humorous way, or whether he
even remembered what I had done.

Waverly looked at me and and shrugged her shoulders.
"You aren't a genius like me," she said matter-of-factly. And
if I hadn't felt so bad, I would have pulled her braids and
punched her stomach.

But my mother's expression was what devastated me: a
quiet, blank look that said she had lost everything. I felt the
same way, and everybody seemed now to be coming up, like
gawkers at the scene of an accident, to see what parts were
actually missing.

When we got on the bus to go home, my father was
humming the busy-bee tune and my mother was silent. I kept
thinking she wanted to wait until we got home before
shouting at me. But when my father unlocked the door to
our apartment, my mother walked in and went straight to
the back, into the bedroom. No accusations. No blame. And
in a way, I felt disappointed. I had been waiting for her to

start shouting, so that I could shout back and cry and blame her for all my misery.

I had assumed that my talent-show fiasco meant that I would never have to play the piano again. But two days later, after school, my mother came out of the kitchen and saw me watching TV.

"Four clock," she reminded me, as if it were any other day. I was stunned, as though she were asking me to go through the talent-show torture again. I planted myself more squarely in front of the TV.

"Turn off TV," she called from the kitchen five minutes later.

I didn't budge. And then I decided. I didn't have to do what my mother said anymore. I wasn't her slave. This wasn't China. I had listened to her before, and look what happened. She was the stupid one.

She came out from the kitchen and stood in the arched entryway of the living room. "Four clock," she said once again, louder.

"I'm not going to play anymore," I said nonchalantly. "Why should I? I'm not a genius."

She stood in front of the TV. I saw that her chest was heaving up and down in an angry way.

"No!" I said, and I now felt stronger, as if my true self had finally emerged. So this was what had been inside me all along.

"No! I won't!" I screamed.

She snapped off the TV, yanked me by the arm and pulled me off the floor. She was frighteningly strong, half pulling, half carrying me toward the piano as I kicked the throw rugs under my feet. She lifted me up and onto the hard bench. I was sobbing by now, looking at her bitterly. Her chest was heaving even more and her mouth was open, smiling crazily as if she were pleased that I was crying.

"You want me to be someone that I'm not!" I sobbed. "I'll never be the kind of daughter you want me to be!"

"Only two kinds of daughters," she shouted in Chinese. "Those who are obedient and those who follow their own mind! Only one kind of daughter can live in this house. Obedient daughter!"

"Then I wish I weren't your daughter. I wish you weren't my mother," I shouted. As I said these things I got scared. It felt like worms and toads and slimy things crawling out of my chest, but it also felt good, that this awful side of me had surfaced, at last.

"Too late change this," my mother said shrilly.

And I could sense her anger rising to its breaking point. I wanted to see it spill over. And that's when I remembered the babies she had lost in China, the ones we never talked about. "Then I wish I'd never been born!" I shouted. "I wish I were dead! Like them."

It was as if I had said magic words. Alakazam! — her face went blank, her mouth closed, her arms went slack, and she backed out of the room, stunned, as if she were blowing away like a small brown leaf, thin, brittle, lifeless.

It was not the only disappointment my mother felt in me. In the years that followed, I failed her many times, each time asserting my will, my right to fall short of expectations. I didn't get straight As. I didn't become class president. I didn't get into Stanford. I dropped out of college.

Unlike my mother, I did not believe I could be anything I wanted to be. I could only be me.

And for all those years we never talked about the disaster at the recital or my terrible declarations afterward at the piano bench. Neither of us talked about it again, as if it were a betrayal that was now unspeakable. So I never found a way to ask her why she had hoped for something so large that failure was inevitable.

And even worse, I never asked her about what frightened me the most: Why had she given up hope? For after our struggle at the piano, she never mentioned my playing again. The lessons stopped. The lid to the piano was closed, shutting out the dust, my misery, and her dreams.

So she surprised me. A few years ago she offered to give me the piano, for my thirtieth birthday. I had not played in all those years. I saw the offer as a sign of forgiveness, a tremendous burden removed.

"Are you sure?" I asked shyly. "I mean, won't you and Dad miss it?"

"No, this your piano," she said firmly. "Always your piano. You only one can play."

"Well, I probably can't play anymore," I said. "It's been years."

"You pick up fast," my mother said, as if she knew this was certain. "You have natural talent. You could be genius if you want to."

"No, I couldn't."

"You just not trying," my mother said. And she was neither angry nor sad. She said it as if announcing a fact that could never be disproved. "Take it," she said.

But I didn't, at first. It was enough that she had offered it to me. And after that, every time I saw it in my parents' living room, standing in front of the bay window, it made me feel proud, as if it were a shiny trophy that I had won back.

Last week I sent a tuner over to my parents' apartment and had the piano reconditioned, for purely sentimental reasons. My mother had died a few months before, and I had been getting things in order for my father, a little bit at a time. I put the jewelry in special silk pouches. The sweaters she had knitted in yellow, pink, bright orange — all the colors I hated — I put in moth-proof boxes. I found some old Chinese silk dresses, the kind with little slits up the sides. I rubbed the old silk against my skin, and then wrapped them in tissue and decided to take them home with me.

After I had the piano tuned, I opened the lid and touched the keys. It sounded even richer than I remembered. Really, it was a very good piano. Inside the bench were the same exercise notes with handwritten scales, the same secondhand music books with their covers held together with yellow tape.

I opened up the Schumann book to the dark little piece I had played at the recital. It was on the left-hand page, "Pleading Child." It looked more difficult than I remembered. I played a few bars, surprised at how easily the notes came back to me.

And for the first time, or so it seemed, I noticed the piece on the right-hand side. It was called "Perfectly Contented." I tried to play this one as well. It had a lighter melody but with the same flowing rhythm and turned out to be quite easy. "Pleading Child" was shorter but slower; "Perfectly Contented" was longer but faster. And after I had played them both a few times, I realized they were two halves of the same song.

WHERE I COME FROM PEOPLE ARE POLITE

William Saroyan

One morning I walked into the office and the bookkeeper was putting on her hat and coat and tears were coming out of her eyes. It was April and what did I care if I was only a fifteen-dollar-a-week clerk in a lousy cemetery company?

Didn't I have a new hat and a new pair of shoes and wasn't the Southern Pacific sending special trains at special low rates down to Monterey every week-end and wasn't I going down to Monterey tomorrow? Wasn't I going to take a train ride down the peninsula tomorrow?

I was going to work until noon Saturday and then I was going to get a deluxe hamburger for fifteen cents at Charley's and then I was going to hurry down to the Southern Pacific depot at Third and Townsend and buy me a special week-end round-trip ticket to Monterey and get on the train and be free in the world from Saturday afternoon till Monday morning. I was going to buy me a copy of the *Saturday Evening Post* and read stories all the way down to Monterey.

When I walked into the office, though, Mrs. Gilpley, the bookkeeper, was putting on her hat and coat and tears were coming out of her eyes.

I stopped whistling and looked around. It was very quiet. The door of Mr. Wylie's office was just a little open, so I figured he was at his desk. Nobody else was around, though. It was twenty minutes past eight, and the clock was making a lot of noise for a clock you could hardly hear ordinarily.

Good morning, Mrs. Gilpley, I said.

Good morning, Joe, she said.

I didn't go straight to the locker and hang up my hat and go to my desk because I knew something was wrong and I figured it wouldn't be polite to just go and hang up my hat

and sit at my desk and not try to understand what was wrong
and why Mrs. Gilpley was putting on her hat and coat and
crying. Mrs. Gilpley was an old lady and she had a mustache
and she was stoop-shouldered and her hands were dry and
full of wrinkles and nobody liked Mrs. Gilpley, but it was
April in the world and I had a new hat and a new pair of
shoes and I had worked in the same office with Mrs. Gilpley
from September till April, right straight through Winter, and
maybe I didn't exactly love her, maybe I wasn't exactly crazy
about her, but she was a good-hearted old lady, and I
couldn't just go and hang up my hat and start another day.
I had to talk to her.

Mrs. Gilpley, I said, is something the matter?

She pointed at the partly open door of Mr. Wylie's private
office and made a sign that told me not to talk and just hang
up my hat and go to work.

I see, I thought. He's fired her.

After all these years.

Mrs. Gilpley, I said, you haven't lost your job, have you?

I've resigned, she said.

No, you haven't, I said. I wasn't born yesterday. You can't
fool me.

Mrs. Gilpley's salary was twenty-seven-fifty per week. It
was eight a week when she first started to work for the
cemetery company. They taught me to do Mrs. Gilpley's
work. My salary was fifteen a week, so they were giving the
old lady the gate. Well, I was pretty lucky to have a job and
I wanted to go down to Monterey and I felt fine in a new
pair of three-dollar shoes and a new hat, but I didn't like the
idea of making Mrs. Gilpley cry at her age.

Mrs. Gilpley, I said, I came in this morning to quit my job
and I'm *going* to quit. I got an uncle in Portland who's
opening a grocery store and I'm going up there to handle his
accounts for him. I ain't going to work for any cemetery
company all my life. I'm quitting.

Joe, Mrs. Gilpley said, you know you ain't got no uncle in Portland.

Is that so? I said. You'd be surprised where I got uncles. I'm through with this job. Keeping track of dead people's addresses. That's some career for a young man.

Joe, Mrs. Gilpley said, if you quit your job, I'll never speak to you again as long as I live.

I don't need no job in a cemetery company, I said. What do I want to be keeping track of dead people for?

You got no friends in this town, Joe, Mrs. Gilpley said. You told me all about where you're from and what you're doing out here in Frisco, and I know how it is. You need this job, and if you quit it, I'll be deeply hurt.

Mrs. Gilpley, I said, how do you think I feel? Coming in here and taking your job? It ain't right. You been doing this work twenty years or more.

Joe, Mrs. Gilpley said, you go on now and hang up your hat and go to work.

I won't, I said. I'm quitting right now.

I walked straight into Mr. Wylie's office. Mr. Wylie was the vice-president. He was an old man with a nose that was squeezed down at the end. He was tall and absent-minded and he wore a derby. And he was mean.

I walked straight into his office. Mr. Wylie, I said, I'm quitting my job beginning this morning.

What's that? he said.

Quitting, I said.

What for? he said.

I ain't getting enough money, I said.

How much do you want? he said.

Boy, was I surprised! I thought he'd throw me out. I figured I'd have to ask for plenty to make him throw me out, so I did.

I want thirty dollars a week, I said.

But you're only eighteen, he said. Such a salary would be a little premature, but perhaps we can arrange it.

If I had tried to put over a thing like that, if I had wanted to put over something like that, and get more money, it never would have worked. Thirty dollars a week was enough to buy me all the stuff I always wanted, in less than six months. Why, I'd be able to buy a Harley-Davidson in no time at thirty a week.

No, I said. I'm quitting.

Why are you quitting? he said. I thought you liked your work?

I used to, I said. But I don't any more. Mr. Wylie, I said, did you fire Mrs. Gilpley?

Mr. Wylie leaned back in his chair and looked at me. He looked sore. Who was I to ask *him* a question like that?

Young man, he said, a check for you will be made out in full this morning. You can come back for it in an hour.

I was sore too.

I want my check *now*, I said.

Then wait in the outer office, he said. Behind the rail.

I went out behind the rail and leaned on the counter.

Mrs. Gilpley looked excited.

I quit, I said.

She couldn't talk.

He wanted to give me thirty dollars a week, I said, but I quit.

She gulped a couple of times.

Mrs. Gilpley, I said, they'll have to give you your job back because they ain't got anybody else to do your work.

Joe, she said, you've hurt me very deeply.

That's all right, I said. Where I come from a young man doesn't take a lady's job. I come from Chicago and I guess I can always go back.

Go back to Chicago? Not me. I liked California. I always liked California. But that's what I said.

Joe, said Mrs. Gilpley, suppose you can't find another job?

I snapped my fingers.

I can get another job just like that, I said.

Mr. Wylie stood in the doorway of his private office and nodded at Mrs. Gilpley and she went into his office and he closed the door. She didn't come out till it was a quarter to nine. She took off her hat and coat and got out the check book and wrote a check and took it to Mr. Wylie.

The check was for me. It was a check for thirteen dollars.

Here's your check, Joe, Mrs. Gilpley said. I tried to get him to give you fifteen, but he said you were insolent.

Did he give you your job back? I said.

Yes, she said.

Mrs. Gilpley, I said, I'm very glad you've got your job back. What did he say I was?

Insolent, said Mrs. Gilpley.

What's that mean? I said.

Impolite, Mrs. Gilpley said.

I ain't impolite, I said. Where I come from people are courteous. Who does he think he's calling impolite?

I went into Mr. Wylie's office and asked him.

Mr. Wylie, I said, who do you think you're calling impolite?

What are you talking about? he said.

You can't call me impolite, I said. Where I come from people are courteous.

People in Chicago aren't really courteous; not in every part of Chicago, but most of the people in the neighborhood where I lived were pretty polite. Most of the time anyway. I guess I was just sore.

You can't say I ain't got good manners, I said.

Where do you come from? Mr. Wylie said.

Chicago, I said. Didn't you know that?

No, he said.

I used to work on South Water Market Street, I said.

Well, said Mr. Wylie, you've got a lot to learn. You're going to learn it doesn't pay to bite the hand that feeds you.

I didn't bite no hand that fed me, I said.

You quit, didn't you? he said.

Yes, sir, I said. I quit all right, but I didn't bite nobody.

Well, what do you want now? he said.

I just want to say goodbye, I said. I just want you to know I've got good manners.

All right, said Mr. Wylie. Goodbye.

Goodbye, I said.

I went out of the office and said goodbye to Mrs. Gilpley. Mr. Wylie came out of his private office while I was saying goodbye to Mrs. Gilpley. She got all excited when he came out of his office, but I wouldn't stop talking.

Mrs. Gilpley, I said, all my life I've wanted to buy a Harley-Davidson and ride around and see a lot of small towns and I guess I could have done it if I had wanted to keep my job here, but where I come from a man don't keep a job and buy a Harley-Davidson and get somebody else who needs a job worse fired.

What's a Harley-Davidson? Mr. Wylie said.

It's a motorcyle, I said.

Oh, he said.

And don't think I won't get along all right, Mrs. Gilpley, I said, because I will.

What do you want with a motorcycle? Mr. Wylie said.

I want to ride it, I said.

What for? he said.

To get somewhere, I said. Travel.

That's no way to travel, Mr. Wylie said.

It's one of the best ways in the world, I said. Mr. Wylie, I don't suppose you've ever driven a motorcycle.

No, I haven't, he said.

There ain't nothing like it, I said. A good motorcycle can go eighty miles an hour, easy.

Mrs. Gilpley, I said, if I ever get a motorcycle with a side-car, I'd be very happy to take you for a little ride through

Golden Gate Park, just to give you an idea how pleasant motorcycle riding can be.

Thank you very much, Joe, Mrs. Gilpley said.

Goodbye, I said.

Goodbye, said Mrs. Gilpley.

Goodbye, said Mr. Wylie.

I went out and rang for the elevator. It was the Greek George.

Where you going? he said.

Portland, I said.

Portland? he said. What you going to do in Portland?

I don't know, I said.

What's the matter? he said.

I just quit my job, I said.

What you want to quit your job for? he said.

I didn't like it, I said. I don't like keeping track of dead people.

You're crazy, he said.

I ain't crazy at all, I said.

I walked out of the elevator, out of the building, and up Market Street. I don't know how it happened, but I went straight to the Harley-Davidson agency, and they showed me the new model. I asked the salesman if I could try one out for a little while, and he talked it over with somebody in an inside office and then he said I could try one out if I would leave some money in the office. In case, he said.

Well, I had the check, so I gave him the check.

It was a beautiful machine. I tore down Market Street and stopped at the building where I used to work and went upstairs and walked into Mr. Wylie's office.

He looked dumbfounded.

Mr. Wylie, I said, I got a beautiful Harley-Davidson downstairs and if you'd like to go for a ride, I'd be more than glad to let you sit behind me. It's a big seat and if I move up toward the front, you'll be comfortable.

I don't want to ride no motorcycle, he said.

I thought maybe you would, I said.

I went out of the office, and then I went back.

Well, would you care to *see* it? I said.

No, he said.

All right, I said, and I went on downstairs and got on the motorcycle and drove away. It was a beautiful job. The motor was great. I got out on the Great Highway at the beach and then I remembered Monterey and I figured maybe I ought to let her out and tear down to Monterey and then tear back, and then give them back their motorcycle and start looking for another job. They'd maybe give me back some of the money, and maybe not, but even if they didn't, I figured it would be worth it, so I let her out. It was the real thing. April. And the Harley-Davidson under me, and the Pacific Ocean beside me. And the world. And the towns. And the people. And the trees. And I roared down to Monterey in no time.

It was a fine town. There were some old buildings in the town, and ships. Fishing ships. There was a fine smell of fish down there, and a lot of sunlight. The fishermen talked very loud in Italian. I drove the Harley-Davidson all around town and right out onto the wet sand of the beach and along the beach for quite a way. I scared a lot of sea gulls and then I stopped at a place and had three hamburgers and two cups of coffee.

Then I started back for Frisco.

It was a great trip, going and coming. It was the most beautiful machine I ever saw. I could do anything with it. I could make it go anywhere, and I did. And I could make it go slower than a man walking, and faster than any expensive car on the highway. I'll bet I passed at least sixty millionaires on the highway. I could make it roar too. I could drive it zig-zag. I could ride it leaning away over on one side. I guess

I scared a lot of people on the highway. I drove it a mile no hands. I stood on the seat a long time, holding the handlebars. People think that's dangerous, but it isn't if you know how to do it.

I had a great time with the Harley-Davidson. Then I took it back and turned it in. The salesman said, Where did you go?

I went down to Monterey, I said.

Monterey? he said. We didn't know you wanted to go that far. We just thought you wanted to find out how it worked.

Well, I said, I always wanted to go down there. Can I have my money back?

Are you going to buy the motorcycle? he said.

How much is it? I said.

It's two hundred and seventy-five dollars, he said.

No, I said. I ain't got that much.

How much have you got? he said.

I got that check, that's all, I said. Them thirteen dollars.

We thought you were going to buy the motorcycle, he said.

I would have bought it if I hadn't quit my job, I said. Can I have my money back?

I don't think so, the salesman said. I'll talk to the manager.

He went into an office and talked, and then he came out and another man was with him. The other man looked important and sore.

What do you mean by taking a new bike and riding it to Monterey and back? he said.

What? I said.

I didn't know what to say. What did *he* mean, *what did I mean?* I didn't mean anything.

You can't do that, he said. We thought you just wanted to ride the motorcycle around the block or show it to somebody or something.

I showed it to a few people, I said. Can I have my money back?

I'm afraid *you* owe *us* money, said the manager. That machine's a new machine. It's for sale. It's second-hand now.

Can't I have *some* of my money back? I said.

No, said the manager.

It's a swell motorcycle, I said.

I walked out of the place and walked up to my room and I didn't even stop to think where I'd ever be able to find a job. I was feeling too happy about the ride to Monterey and back.

LOST SISTER

Dorothy M. Johnson

Our household was full of women, who overwhelmed my
Uncle Charlie and sometimes confused me with their bustle
and chatter. We were the only men on the place. I was nine
years old when still another woman came — Aunt Bessie,
who had been living with the Indians.

When my mother told me about her, I couldn't believe it.
The savages had killed my father, a cavalry lieutenant, two
years before. I hated Indians and looked forward to wiping
them out when I got older. (But when I was grown, they were
no menace anymore.)

"What did she live with the hostiles for?" I demanded.

"They captured her when she was a little girl," Ma said.
"She was three years younger than you are. Now she's
coming home."

High time she came home, I thought. I said so, promising,
"If they was ever to get me, I wouldn't stay with 'em long."

Ma put her arms around me. "Don't talk like that. They
won't get you. They'll never get you."

I was my mother's only real tie with her husband's family.
She was not happy with those masterful women, my Aunts
Margaret, Hannah and Sabina, but she would not go back
East where she came from. Uncle Charlie managed the store
the aunts owned, but he wasn't really a member of the
family — he was just Aunt Margaret's husband. The only
man who had belonged was my father, the aunts' younger
brother. And I belonged, and someday the store would be
mine. My mother stayed to protect my heritage.

None of the three sisters, my aunts, had ever seen Aunt
Bessie. She had been taken by the Indians before they were
born. Aunt Mary had known her — Aunt Mary was two

years older — but she lived a thousand miles away now and was not well.

There was no picture of the little girl who had become a legend. When the family had first settled here, there was enough struggle to feed and clothe the children without having pictures made of them.

Even after Army officers had come to our house several times and there had been many letters about Aunt Bessie's delivery from the savages, it was a long time before she came. Major Harris, who made the final arrangements, warned my aunts that they would have problems, that Aunt Bessie might not be able to settle down easily into family life.

This was only a challenge to Aunt Margaret, who welcomed challenges. "She's our own flesh and blood," Aunt Margaret trumpeted. "Of course she must come to us. My poor, dear sister Bessie, torn from her home forty years ago!"

The major was earnest but not tactful. "She's been with the savages all those years," he insisted. "And she was only a little girl when she was taken. I haven't seen her myself, but it's reasonable to assume that she'll be like an Indian woman."

My stately Aunt Margaret arose to show that the audience was ended. "Major Harris," she intoned, "I cannot permit anyone to criticize my own dear sister. She will live in my home, and if I do not receive official word that she is coming within a month, I shall take steps."

Aunt Bessie came before the month was up.

The aunts in residence made valiant preparations. They bustled and swept and mopped and polished. They moved me from my own room to my mother's — as she had been begging them to do because I was troubled with nightmares. They prepared my old room for Aunt Bessie with many small comforts — fresh doilies everywhere, hairpins, a matching pitcher and bowl, the best towels and two new nightgowns in case hers might be old. (The fact was that she didn't have any.)

"Perhaps we should have some dresses made," Hannah suggested. "We don't know what she'll have with her."

"We don't know what size she'll take, either," Margaret pointed out. "There'll be time enough for her to go to the store after she settles down and rests for a day or two. Then she can shop to her heart's content."

Ladies of the town came to call almost every afternoon while the preparations were going on. Margaret promised them that, as soon as Bessie had recovered sufficiently from her ordeal, they should all meet her at tea.

Margaret warned her anxious sisters, "Now, girls, we mustn't ask her too many questions at first. She must rest for a while. She's been through a terrible experience." Margaret's voice dropped way down with those last two words, as if only she could be expected to understand.

Indeed Bessie had been through a terrible experience, but it wasn't what the sisters thought. The experience from which she was suffering, when she arrived, was that she had been wrenched from her people, the Indians, and turned over to strangers. She had not been freed. She had been made a captive.

Aunt Bessie came with Major Harris and an interpreter, a half-blood with greasy black hair hanging down to his shoulders. His costume was half Army and half primitive. Aunt Margaret swung the door open wide when she saw them coming. She ran out with her sisters following, while my mother and I watched from a window. Margaret's arms were outstretched, but when she saw the woman closer, her arms dropped and her glad cry died.

She did not cringe, my Aunt Bessie who had been an Indian for forty years, but she stopped walking and stood staring, helpless among her captors.

The sisters had described her often as a little girl. Not that they had ever seen her, but she was a legend, the captive child. Beautiful blonde curls, they said she had, and big blue eyes — she was a fairy child, a pale-haired little angel who ran on dancing feet.

The Bessie who came back was an aging woman who plodded in moccasins, whose dark dress did not belong on her bulging body. Her brown hair hung just below her ears. It was growing out; when she was first taken from the Indians, her hair had been cut short to clean out the vermin.

Aunt Margaret recovered herself and, instead of embracing this silent stolid woman, satisfied herself by patting an arm and crying, "Poor dear Bessie, I am your sister Margaret. And here are our sisters Hannah and Sabina. We do hope you're not all tired out from your journey!"

Aunt Margaret was all graciousness, because she had been assured beyond doubt that this was truly a member of the family. She must have believed — Aunt Margaret could believe anything — that all Bessie needed was to have a nice nap and wash her face. Then she would be as talkative as any of them.

The other aunts were quick-moving and sharp of tongue. But this one moved as if her sorrows were a burden on her bowed shoulders, and when she spoke briefly in answer to the interpreter, you could not understand a word of it.

Aunt Margaret ignored these peculiarities. She took the party into the front parlor — even the interpreter, when she understood there was no avoiding it. She might have gone on battling with the major about him, but she was in a hurry to talk to her lost sister.

"You won't be able to converse with her unless the interpreter is present," Major Harris said. "Not," he explained hastily, "because of any regulation, but because she has forgotten English."

Aunt Margaret gave the half-blood interpreter a look of

frowning doubt and let him enter. She coaxed Bessie. "Come, dear, sit down."

The interpreter mumbled, and my Indian aunt sat cautiously on a needlepoint chair. For most of her life she had been living with people who sat comfortably on the ground. The visit in the parlor was brief. Bessie had had her instructions before she came. But Major Harris had a few warnings for the family. "Technically, your sister is still a prisoner," he explained, ignoring Margaret's start of horror. "She will be in your custody. She may walk in your fenced yard, but she must not leave it without official permission.

"Mrs. Raleigh, this may be a heavy burden for you all. But she has been told all this and has expressed willingness to conform to these restrictions. I don't think you will have any trouble keeping her here." Major Harris hesitated, remembered that he was a soldier and a brave man, and added, "If I did, I wouldn't have brought her."

There was the making of a sharp little battle, but Aunt Margaret chose to overlook the challenge. She could not overlook the fact that Bessie was not what she had expected.

Bessie certainly knew that this was her lost white family, but she didn't seem to care. She was infinitely sad, infinitely removed. She asked one question: "Mary?" and Aunt Margaret almost wept with joy.

"Sister Mary lives a long way from here," she explained, "and she isn't well, but she will come as soon as she's able. Dear sister Mary!"

The interpreter translated this, and Bessie had no more to say. That was the only understandable word she ever did say in our house, the remembered name of her older sister.

When the aunts, all chattering, took Bessie to her room, one of them asked, "But where are her things?"

Bessie had no things, no baggage. She had nothing at all but the clothes she stood in. While the sisters scurried to bring a comb and other oddments, she stood like a stooped

monument, silent and watchful. This was her prison. Very
well, she would endure it.

"Maybe tomorrow we can take her to the store and see
what she would like," Aunt Hannah suggested.

"There's no hurry," Aunt Margaret declared thoughtfully.
She was getting the idea that this sister was going to be a
problem. But I don't think Aunt Margaret ever really stopped
hoping that one day Bessie would cease to be different, that
she would end her stubborn silence and begin to relate the
events of her life among the savages, in the parlor over a cup
of tea.

My Indian aunt accustomed herself, finally, to sitting on
the chair in her room. She seldom came out, which was a
relief to her sisters. She preferred to stand, hour after hour,
looking out the window — which was open only about a
foot, in spite of all Uncle Charlie's efforts to budge it higher.
And she always wore moccasins. She was never able to wear
shoes from the store, but seemed to treasure the shoes
brought to her.

The aunts did not, of course, take her shopping after all.
They made her a couple of dresses; and when they told her,
with signs and voluble explanations, to change her dress, she
did.

After I found that she was usually at the window, looking
across the flat land to the blue mountains, I played in the
yard so I could stare at her. She never smiled, as an aunt
should, but she looked at me sometimes, thoughtfully, as if
measuring my worth. By performing athletic feats, such as
walking on my hands, I could get her attention. For some
reason, I valued it.

She didn't often change expression, but twice I saw her
scowl with disapproval. Once was when one of the aunts
slapped me in a casual way. I had earned the slap, but the
Indians did not punish children with blows. Aunt Bessie was
shocked, I think, to see that white people did. The other time

was when I talked back to someone with spoiled, small-boy insolence — and that time the scowl was for me.

The sisters and my mother took turns, as was their Christian duty, in visiting her for half an hour each day. Bessie didn't eat at the table with us — not after the first meal.

The first time my mother took her turn, it was under protest. "I'm afraid I'd start crying in front of her," she argued, but Aunt Margaret insisted.

I was lurking in the hall when Ma went in. Bessie said something, then said it again, peremptorily, until my mother guessed what she wanted. She called me and put her arm around me as I stood beside her chair. Aunt Bessie nodded, and that was all there was to it.

Afterward, my mother said, "She likes you. And so do I." She kissed me.

"I don't like her," I complained. "She's queer."

"She's a sad old lady," my mother explained. "She had a little boy once, you know."

"What happened to him?"

"He grew up and became a warrior. I suppose she was proud of him. Now the Army has him in prison somewhere. He's half Indian. He was a dangerous man."

He was indeed a dangerous man, and a proud man, a chief, a bird of prey whose wings the Army had clipped after bitter years of trying.

However, my mother and my Indian aunt had that one thing in common: they both had sons. The other aunts were childless.

There was a great to-do about having Aunt Bessie's photograph taken. The aunts who were stubbornly and valiantly trying to make her one of the family wanted a picture of her for the family album. The government wanted one too, for some reason — perhaps because someone realized that a thing of historic importance had been accomplished by recovering the captive child.

Major Harris sent a young lieutenant with the greasy-haired interpreter to discuss the matter in the parlor. (Margaret, with great foresight, put a clean towel on a chair and saw to it the interpreter sat there.) Bessie spoke very little during that meeting, and of course we understood only what the half-blood *said* she was saying.

No, she did not want her picture made. No.

But your son had his picture made. Do you want to see it? They teased her with that offer, and she nodded.

If we let you see his picture, then will you have yours made?

She nodded doubtfully. Then she demanded more than had been offered: If you let me keep his picture, then you can make mine.

No, you can only look at it. We have to keep his picture. It belongs to us.

My Indian aunt gambled for high stakes. She shrugged and spoke, and the interpreter said, "She not want to look. She will keep or nothing."

My mother shivered, understanding as the aunts could not understand what Bessie was gambling — all or nothing.

Bessie won. Perhaps they had intended that she should. She was allowed to keep the photograph that had been made of her son. It has been in history books many times — the half-white chief, the valiant leader who was not quite great enough to keep his Indian people free.

His photograph was taken after he was captured, but you would never guess it. His head is high, his eyes stare with boldness but not with scorn, his long hair is arranged with care — dark hair braided on one side and with a tendency to curl where the other side hangs loose — and his hands hold the pipe like a royal scepter.

That photograph of the captive but unconquered warrior had its effect on me. Remembering him, I began to control my temper and my tongue, to cultivate reserve as I grew older, to stare with boldness but not scorn at people who annoyed or offended me. I never met him, but I took silent pride in him — Eagle Head, my Indian cousin.

Bessie kept his picture on her dresser when she was not holding it in her hands. And she went like a docile, silent child to the photograph studio, in a carriage with Aunt Margaret early one morning, when there would be few people on the street to stare.

Bessie's photograph is not proud but pitiful. She looks out with no expression. There is no emotion there, no challenge, only the face of an aging woman with short hair, only endurance and patience. The aunts put a copy in the family album.

But they were nearing the end of their tether. The Indian aunt was a solid ghost in the house. She did nothing because there was nothing for her to do. Her gnarled hands must have been skilled at squaws' work, at butchering meat and scraping and tanning hides, at making tepees and beading ceremonial clothes. But her skills were useless and unwanted in a civilized home. She did not even sew when my mother gave her cloth and needles and thread. She kept the sewing things beside her son's picture.

She ate (in her room) and slept (on the floor) and stood looking out the window. That was all, and it could not go on. But it had to go on, at least until my sick Aunt Mary was well enough to travel — Aunt Mary who was her older sister, the only one who had known her when they were children.

The sisters' duty visits to Aunt Bessie became less and less visits and more and more duty. They settled into a bearable routine. Margaret had taken upon herself the responsibility of trying to make Bessie talk. Make, I said, not teach. She firmly believed that her stubborn and unfortunate sister needed only encouragement from a strong-willed person. So Margaret talked, as to a child, when she bustled in:

"Now there you stand, just looking, dear. What in the world is there to see out there? The birds — are you watching the birds? Why don't you try sewing? Or you could go for a little walk in the yard. Don't you want to go out for a nice little walk?"

Bessie listened and blinked.

Margaret could have understood an Indian woman's not being able to converse in a civilized tongue, but her own sister was not an Indian. Bessie was white, therefore she should talk the language her sisters did — the language she had not heard since early childhood.

Hannah, the put-upon aunt, talked to Bessie too, but she was delighted not to get any answers and not to be interrupted. She bent over her embroidery when it was her turn to sit with Bessie and told her troubles in an unending flow. Bessie stood looking out the window the whole time.

Sabina, who had just as many troubles, most of them emanating from Margaret and Hannah, went in like a martyr, firmly clutching her Bible, and read aloud from it until her time was up. She took a small clock along so that she would not, because of annoyance, be tempted to cheat.

After several weeks Aunt Mary came, white and trembling and exhausted from her illness and the long, hard journey. The sisters tried to get the interpreter in but were not successful. (Aunt Margaret took that failure pretty hard.) They briefed Aunt Mary, after she had rested, so the shock of seeing Bessie would not be too terrible. I saw them meet, those two.

Margaret went to the Indian woman's door and explained volubly who had come, a useless but brave attempt. Then she stood aside, and Aunt Mary was there, her lined white face aglow, her arms outstretched. "Bessie! Sister Bessie!" she cried.

And after one brief moment's hesitation, Bessie went into her arms and Mary kissed her sun-dark, weathered cheek.

Bessie spoke. "Ma-ry," she said. "Ma-ry." She stood with tears running down her face and her mouth working. So much to tell, so much suffering and fear — and joy and triumph, too — and the sister there at last who might legitimately hear it all and understand.

But the only English word that Bessie remembered was "Mary," and she had not cared to learn any others. She turned to the dresser, took her son's picture in her work-hardened hands, reverently, and held it so her sister could see. Her eyes pleaded.

Mary looked on the calm, noble, savage face of her half-blood nephew and said the right thing: "My, isn't he handsome!" She put her head on one side and then the other. "A fine boy, sister," she approved. "You must" — she stopped, but she finished — "be awfully proud of him, dear!"

Bessie understood the tone if not the words. The tone was admiration. Her son was accepted by the sister who mattered. Bessie looked at the picture and nodded, murmuring. Then she put it back on the dresser.

Aunt Mary did not try to make Bessie talk. She sat with her every day for hours and Bessie did talk — but not in English. They sat holding hands for mutual comfort while the captive child, grown old and a grandmother, told what had happened in forty years. Aunt Mary said that was what Bessie was talking about. But she didn't understand a word of it and didn't need to.

"There is time enough for her to learn English again," Aunt Mary said. "I think she understands more than she lets on. I asked her if she'd like to come and live with me, and she nodded. We'll have the rest of our lives for her to learn English. But what she has been telling me — she can't wait to tell that. About her life, and her son."

"Are you sure, Mary dear, that you should take the responsibility of having her?" Margaret asked dutifully, no doubt shaking in her shoes for fear Mary would change her mind now that deliverance was in sight. "I do believe she'd be happier with you, though we've done all we could."

Margaret and the other sisters would certainly be happier with Bessie somewhere else. And so, it developed, would the United States government.

Major Harris came with the interpreter to discuss details, and they told Bessie she could go, if she wished, to live with Mary a thousand miles away. Bessie was patient and willing, stolidly agreeable. She talked a great deal more to the interpreter than she had ever done before. He answered at length and then explained to the others that she wanted to know how she and Mary would travel to this far country. It was hard, he said, for her to understand just how far they were going.

Later we knew that the interpreter and Bessie had talked about much more than that.

Next morning, when Sabina took breakfast to Bessie's room, we heard a cry of dismay. Sabina stood holding the tray, repeating, "She's gone out the window! She's gone out the window!"

And so she had. The window that had always stuck so that it would not raise more than a foot was open wider now. And the photograph of Bessie's son was gone from the dresser. Nothing else was missing except Bessie and the decent dark dress she had worn the day before.

My Uncle Charlie got no breakfast that morning. With Margaret shrieking orders, he leaped on a horse and rode to the telegraph station.

Before Major Harris got there with half a dozen cavalrymen, civilian scouts were out searching for the missing woman. They were expert trackers. Their lives had depended, at various times, on their ability to read the meaning of a turned stone, a broken twig, a bruised leaf. They found that Bessie had gone south. They tracked her for ten miles. And then they lost the trail, for Bessie was as skilled as they were.

Her life had sometimes depended on leaving no stone or twig or leaf marked by her passage. She traveled fast at first. Then, with time to be careful, she evaded the followers she knew would come.

The aunts were stricken with grief — at least Aunt Mary was — and bowed with humiliation about what Bessie had done. The blinds were drawn, and voices were low in the house. We had been pitied because of Bessie's tragic folly in having let the Indians make a savage of her. But now we were traitors because we had let her get away.

Aunt Mary kept saying pitifully, "Oh, why did she go? I thought she would be contented with me!"

The others said that it was, perhaps, all for the best.

Aunt Margaret proclaimed, "She has gone back to her own." That was what they honestly believed, and so did Major Harris.

My mother told me why she had gone. "You know that picture she had of the Indian chief, her son? He's escaped from the jail he was in. The fort got word of it, and they think Bessie may be going to where he's hiding. That's why they're trying so hard to find her. They think," my mother explained, "that she knew of his escape before they did. They think the interpreter told her when he was here. There was no other way she could have found out."

They scoured the mountains to the south for Eagle Head and Bessie. They never found her, and they did not get him until a year later, far to the north. They could not capture him that time. He died fighting.

After I grew up, I operated the family store, disliking storekeeping a little more every day. When I was free to sell it, I did, and went to raising cattle. And one day, riding in a canyon after strayed steers, I found — I think — Aunt Bessie. A cowboy who worked for me was along, or I would never have let anybody know.

We found weathered bones near a little spring. They had

a mystery on them, those nameless human bones suddenly come upon. I could feel old death brushing my back.

"Some prospector," suggested my riding partner.

I thought so too until I found, protected by a log, sodden scraps of fabric that might have been a dark, respectable dress. And wrapped in them was a sodden something that might have once been a picture.

The man with me was young, but he had heard the story of the captive child. He had been telling me about it, in fact. In the passing years it had acquired some details that surprised me. Aunt Bessie had become once more a fair-haired beauty, in this legend that he had heard, but utterly sad and silent. Well, sad and silent she really was.

I tried to push the sodden scrap of fabric back under the log, but he was too quick for me. "That ain't no shirt, that's a dress!" he announced. "This here was no prospector — it was a woman!" He paused and then announced with awe, "I bet you it was your Indian aunt!"

I scowled and said, "Nonsense. It could be anybody."

He got all worked up about it. "If it was *my* aunt," he declared, "I'd bury her in the family plot."

"No," I said, and shook my head.

We left the bones there in the canyon, where they had been for forty-odd years if they were Aunt Bessie's. And I think they were. But I would not make her a captive again. She's in the family album. She doesn't need to be in the family plot.

If my guess about why she left us is wrong, nobody can prove it. She never intended to join her son in hiding. She went in the opposite direction to lure pursuit away.

What happened to her in the canyon doesn't concern me, or anyone. My Aunt Bessie accomplished what she set out to do. It was not her life that mattered, but his. She bought him another year.

THE NEW MIRROR

Ann Petry

My mother said, "Where is your father?" She was standing outside the door of the downstairs bathroom. Even if she had been farther away, I would have understood what she said, because her voice had a peculiar quality just this side of harshness, which made it carry over longer distances than other people's voices.

From inside the bathroom, I said, "He's in the back yard listening to the bees."

"Please tell him that breakfast is ready."

"Right away," I said. But I didn't tell him right away. I didn't move. We had had a late, cold spring, with snow on the ground until the end of April. Then in May the weather turned suddenly warm and the huge old cherry trees in our yard blossomed almost overnight. There were three of them, planted in a straight line down the middle of the back yard. As soon as the sun was up, it seemed as though all the honeybees in Wheeling, New York, came to the trees in swarms. Every sunny morning, my father stood under one of those bloom-filled cherry trees and listened to the hum of the bees. My mother knew this just as well as I did, but she was sending a bathroom dawdler to carry a message to a cherry-tree dawdler so that she would finally have both of us in the dining room for breakfast at the same time.

I spent the next ten minutes looking at myself in the new plate-glass mirror that had been hung over the basin just the day before. A new electrical fixture had been installed over the mirror. My mother had had these changes made so that my father could shave downstairs. She said this would be more convenient for him, because it placed him closer to the drugstore while he shaved. Our drugstore was in the front of the building where we lived.

The bathroom walls were white, and under the brilliant, all-revealing light cast by the new fixture I looked like all dark creatures impaled on a flat white surface: too big, too dark. My skin was a muddy brown, not the clear, dark brown I had always supposed it to be. I turned my head and the braid of hair that reached halfway down my back looked like a thick black snake. It even undulated slightly as I moved. I grabbed the braid close to my head and looked around for a pair of scissors, thinking I would cut the braid off, because it was an absolutely revolting hair style for a fifteen-year-old girl. But there weren't any scissors, so I released my grip on the braid and took another look at myself — head-on in the glittering mirror. I decided that the way I looked in that white-walled bathroom was the way our family looked in the town of Wheeling, New York. We were the only admittedly black family in an all-white community and we stood out; we looked strange, alien. There was another black family — the Granites — but they claimed to be Mohawk Indians. Whenever my father mentioned them, he laughed until tears came to his eyes, saying, "Mohawks? Ha, ha, ha. Well, five or six generations of Fanti tribesmen must have caught five or six generations of those Mohawk females named Granite under a bush somewhere. Ha, ha, ha."

He never said things like that in the drugstore. He and my mother and my aunts kept their private lives and their thoughts about people inside the family circle, deliberately separating the life of the family from the life of the drugstore. But it didn't work the other way around, for practically everything we did was decided in terms of whether it was good or bad for the drugstore. I liked the store, and I liked working in it on Saturdays and after school, but it often seemed to me a monstrous, mindless, sightless force that shaped our lives into any old pattern it chose, and it chose the patterns at random.

I turned out the light and went to tell my father that breakfast was ready. He was standing motionless under the first big cherry tree. He had his back turned, but I could tell from the way he held his head that he was listening intently. He was short, and seen from the back like that, his torso looked as though it had been designed for a bigger man.

"Yoo-hoo!" I shouted, as though I were calling someone at least two hundred feet away from me. "Break-fast. Break-fast." In my mind, I said, "Sam-u-el, Sam-u-el." But I didn't say that out loud.

He did not turn around. He lifted his hand in a gesture that pushed the sound of my voice away, indicating that he had heard me and that I was not to call him again.

I sat down on the back steps to wait for him. Though the sun was up, it was cool in the yard. The air was filled with a delicate fragrance that came from all the flowering shrubs, from the cherry blossoms and the pear blossoms, and from the small plants — violets and daffodils. A song sparrow was singing somewhere close by. I told myself that if I were a maker of perfumes I would make one and call it "Spring," and it would smell like this cool, sweet, early-morning air and I would let only beautiful young brown girls use it, and if I could sing I would sing like the song sparrow and I would let only beautiful young brown boys hear me.

When we finally went into the house and sat down to breakfast, my father said (just as he did every spring) that the honeybees buzzed on one note and that it was E-flat just below middle C but with a difference. He said he had never been able to define this in the musical part of his mind and so had decided that it was the essential difference in the sound produced by the buzzing of a bee and the sound produced by a human voice lifted in song. He also said that he wouldn't want to live anywhere else in the world except right here in Wheeling, New York, in the building that housed our drugstore, with that big back yard with those

cherry trees in it, so that in the spring of the year, when the
trees were in full bloom, he could stand under them smelling
that cherry-blossom sweet air and listening to those bees
holding that one note — E-flat below middle C. Then he said,
"When I was out there just now, that first cherry tree was so
aswarm with life, there were so many bees moving around
bumping into the blossoms and making that buzzing sound,
that hum . . ." He touched his forehead lightly with one of
his big hands, as though he were trying to stimulate his
thinking processes. "You know, I could have sworn that tree
spoke to me."

I leaned toward him, waiting to hear what he was going
to say. I did not believe the tree had said anything to him,
but I wanted to know what it was he *thought* the tree had
said. It seemed to me a perfect moment for this kind of
revelation. We had just finished eating an enormous breakfast: grapefruit and oatmeal and scrambled eggs and sausage
and hot cornmeal muffins. This delicious food and this sunny
room in which we had eaten it were pleasant segments of the
private part of our life, totally separated from the drugstore,
which was the public part. I relished the thought that the
steady stream of white customers who went in and out of
our drugstore did not know what our dining room was like,
did not even know if we had one. It was like having a
concealed weapon to use against your enemy.

The dining room was a square-shaped, white-walled room
on the east side of the building. The brilliant light of the
morning sun was reflected from the walls so that the whole
room seemed to shimmer with light and the walls were no
longer white but a pale yellow. I thought my father looked
quite handsome in this room. His skin was a deep reddish
brown and he was freshly shaved. He had used an after-shave
lotion, and it gave his face a shiny look. He was bald-headed,
and in this brilliantly sunlit room the skin on his face and on
his head looked as though it had been polished.

The dining room table was oak. It was square, well suited to the square shape of the room. The chairs had tall backs and there was a design across the top of each one. The design looked as though it had been pressed into the wood by some kind of machine.

My mother sat at one end of the table and my father sat at the other end, in armchairs. I sat on one side of the table, and my Aunt Sophronia sat on the other side. She was my mother's youngest sister. She and my mother looked very much alike, though she was lighter in color than my mother. They were both short, rather small-boned women. Their eyes looked black, though they were a very dark brown. They wore their hair the same way — piled up on top of their heads. My mother's hair was beginning to turn gray, but Aunt Sophronia's was black. There was a big difference in their voices. Aunt Sophronia's voice was low-pitched, musical — a very gentle voice.

My aunt and my mother and father were drinking their second cups of coffee and I was drinking my second glass of milk when my father said he thought the cherry tree had spoken to him. They both looked at him in surprise.

I asked, "What did the tree say?"

"It bent down toward me and it said . . ." He paused, beckoned to me to lean toward him a little more. He lowered his voice. "The tree said, 'Child of the sun — '" He stopped talking and looked directly at me. In that sun-washed room, his eyes were reddish brown, almost the same color as his skin, and I got the funny feeling that I had never really looked right at him before, and that he believed the tree had said something to him, and I was shocked. He whispered, "The tree said, 'It will soon be time to go and open the drugstore!'"

I scowled at him and he threw his head back and laughed, making a roaring, explosive sound. It was just as though he had said, "Got you, you idiot — you — ha, ha, ha." He

opened his mouth so wide I could see his gums, red and
moist, see the three teeth that he had left, one in the upper
jaw and two in the lower jaw, even see his tonsils. I began
muttering to him in my mind, "How do you chew your food,
old toothless one with the red-brown skin and the bald head.
Go up, thou bald head. Go up, thou bald-headed black
man."

Right after breakfast, I helped my father open the
drugstore for the day. I was still annoyed that he had been
able to fool me into thinking he believed a cherry tree had
spoken to him, but I so enjoyed working in the drugstore
that I would not deny myself that pleasure simply because he
had deliberately talked nonsense and I had been stupid
enough to believe him.

He swept the floor with a big soft-bristled broom. Then he
went outside and swept off the long, wooden steps that ran
all the way across the front of the building. He left the front
door open, and the cool, sweet-smelling early-morning air
dispelled the heavy odor of cigars, the sticky vanilla smell
from the soda fountain and the medicinal smell of the
prescription room — part alcohol, part spicy things, part dis-
infectant.

I put change in both the cash registers — the one in the
store proper and the one behind the fountain. The fountain
was in a separate room, rather like a porch with a great
many windows. I put syrups in the fountain — chocolate,
Coca-Cola, root beer, lemon, cherry, vanilla. The chocolate
syrup had a mouth-watering smell, and the cherry and the
lemon syrups smelled like a fruit stand on a hot summer day,
but the root beer and the Coca-Cola syrups smelled like
metal.

Our black and white cat sat in the doorway and watched
my father. The cat yawned, opening his mouth wide, and I
could see his wonderful flexible pink tongue and his teeth —

like the teeth of a tiger, only smaller, of course. I wondered
if cats ever became practically toothless, like my father. He
wouldn't have cavities filled because he said all that silver or
amalgam or gold or whatever it was, and all that X-raying
that butter-fingered dentists do, and all that use of Novocain
was what made people develop cancer of the jaw. When his
teeth hurt and the dentist said the pain was due to a big
cavity, he simply had the tooth pulled out without an
anesthetic. Once I asked him if it hurt to have teeth pulled
without Novocain or gas. He said, "Of course it hurts. But
it is a purely temporary hurt. The roots of my teeth go
straight down and it is a very simple matter to pull them out.
I've pulled some of them out myself."

I sorted the newspapers, looked at the headlines, quickly
skimmed the inside of the Buffalo *News*. I saw a picture of
a man, obviously an actor, wearing a straw hat. I wanted the
picture because of his tooth-revealing grin, and I reminded
myself to cut it out. The newspapers that didn't sell were
returned for credit. Quite often I snipped out items that
interested me. I always hunted for articles that dealt with the
importance of chewing food thoroughly, and for pictures of
men with no teeth, and for pictures of very handsome men
exposing a great many teeth. I intended to leave this
particular picture on the prescription counter, where my
father would be sure to see it.

When Aunt Sophronia came to work at nine o'clock, the
store was clean and it smelled good inside. Like my father,
she was a pharmacist, and when he was not in the store, she
was there. She wore dark skirts and white shirtwaists when
she was working, and she put on a gray cotton store coat so
that people would know she worked in the store and would
not think she was a customer.

One other person worked in the drugstore — Pedro, a
twelve-year-old Portuguese boy. He was supposed to arrive
at nine on Saturdays and Sundays. He was always prompt

and the first stroke of the town clock had not yet sounded
when he came hurrying into the store. He was a very sturdily
built boy, with big dark eyes. He had an enormous quantity
of tangled black hair. He couldn't afford to have his hair cut
at the barbershop, so my father cut it for him. The first time
I saw him cutting Pedro's hair out in the back room, I asked
him if he knew how to cut hair.

He said, "No."

I said, "Well, how do you know what to do?"

"I don't," he said, snipping away with the scissors. "But I
can shorten it some. Otherwise, he'll look like a girl."

Though Pedro was fond of all of us, he had a special feeling
about my father. He told my father that he would like to stay
in the store all the time — he could sleep in the back room,
and all he needed was a blanket and a mattress and he could
bring those from home, and he would provide his own food
and clothes. There were eleven kids in his family, and I
imagine he preferred being part of a family in which there
were fewer people, and so decided to become a member of
our family. My father wouldn't let him sleep in the back
room, but Pedro did manage to spend most of his waking
hours (when he wasn't in school, of course) at the store. He
provided his own food. He ate oranges, sucking out the juice
and the pulp. He hung a big smoked sausage from one of the
rafters in the back room and sliced off pieces of it for his
lunch. He loved fresh pineapple, and he was always saying
that the only thing in the world he'd ever steal if he couldn't
get it any other way would be a ripe pineapple.

At one minute after nine, my father went to the post office.
When he left, he was holding some letters that he was going
to mail. I thought his hand looked big and very dark holding
all those white envelopes. I went to the door and watched
him as he walked up the street, past the elm trees, past the
iron urn on the village green, past the robins and the tender
green young grass on each side of the gravel path. He had a

stiff straw hat tilted just a little toward the back of his head. As he moved off up the street, he was whistling "Ain't goin' to study war no more, no more, no more."

We were so busy in the store that morning that I did not realize what time it was until my mother called up to find out why my father had not been home for his noon meal. There was such a sharp line of demarcation between house and store that my mother always telephoned the drugstore when she had a message for my father.

Aunt Sophronia answered the phone. I heard her say, "He's not in the store right now — he's probably in the cellar. We'll send him right along." After she hung up the receiver, she said, "See if your father is in the cellar unpacking stock or way down in the yard burning rubbish."

He wasn't in the cellar and he wasn't in the back yard. The burner was piled high with the contents of the wastebasket from the prescription room (junk mail, empty pillboxes, old labels) and the contents of the rubbish box from the fountain (straws, paper napkins, Popsicle wrappers).

All three cherry trees were still filled with bees, and they were buzzing on their one note. I walked from one tree to the next, pausing to listen, looking up into the white blossoms, and the trees seemed to be alive in a strange way because of the comings and goings of the bees. As I stood there, I felt it would be very easy to believe that those trees could speak to me.

I went back to the drugstore, and Aunt Sophronia said, "You didn't see him?"

"No. And I don't think he ever came back from the post office. Each time someone asked for him, I thought he was in the back room or down in the cellar or outside in the yard. And each time, whoever it was wanted him said they'd come back later, and I never really had to look for him."

"I'll call the post office and ask if he's picked up our packages, and that way I'll find out if he's been there without actually saying that we're looking for him."

I could hear her end of the conversation, and obviously he hadn't been in the post office at all that morning. She hung up the telephone and called the railroad station and asked if Mr. Layen had been there to get an express package. The stationmaster had a big booming voice, and I could hear him say, "No." Aunt Sophronia said, "You would have seen him if he had been at the station?" He said, "I certainly would."

Pedro and I wanted to go and look for my father. Aunt Sophronia snapped at us, saying, "Don't be foolish. Where would you look? In the river? In the taverns? Your father wouldn't kill himself, and he doesn't drink. . . ."

She frightened me. She had frightened Pedro, too; he was pale and his eyes looked bigger. I had thought my father was late for dinner because he had stopped somewhere to talk and got involved in a long-winded conversation, and that if Pedro and I had walked up or down the street we would have found him and told him his dinner was ready. Aunt Sophronia obviously thought something dreadful had happened to him. Now we began to think so, too.

We kept waiting on the customers just as though there was no crisis in our family. I kept saying to myself, "Your father dies, your mother dies, you break your leg or your back, you stand in a pool of cold sweat from a fever, you stand in a pool of warm blood from a wound, and you go out in the store and smile and say, 'Fine, just fine, we're all fine, nothin's ever wrong with us cull-ed folks.'"

Whenever the store was empty, my aunt would say nervously, "What could have happened to him?" And then clear her throat two or three times in quick succession — a sure sign that she was upset and frightened. Later in the afternoon she said in a queer way, just as though he had passed out of our lives and she was already reminiscing about him, "He did everything at exactly the same time every day.

He always said that was the only way you could run a store — have a certain time for everything and stick to it." This was true. He opened the drugstore promptly at eight, he went to get the mail promptly at nine, and he ate his dinner at twelve. At four in the afternoon, he drank a bottle of Moxie — the only soda pop that he regarded as fit for human consumption. (He said if that were ever taken off the market he would have to drink tea, which upset his stomach because it was a drink suited to the emotional needs of the Chinese, the East Indians, the English, the Irish, and nervous American females, and it had, therefore, no value for him, representing as he did a segment of a submerged population group only a few generations out of Africa, where his ancestors had obviously been witch doctors.)

On Sundays he went to church. He went in through the rear entrance and into the choir loft from the back about two minutes after the service started. There was a slight stir as the ladies of the choir and the other male singer (a tall, thin man who sang bass) rearranged themselves to make room for him. He sang a solo almost every Sunday, for he had a great big, beautiful tenor voice. On Sundays he smelled strongly of after-shave lotion, and on weekdays he smelled faintly of after-shave lotion.

My aunt kept saying, "Where would he go? Where would he go?"

I said, "Maybe he went to Buffalo." I didn't believe this, but she'd have to stop clearing her throat long enough to contradict me.

"What would he go there for? Why wouldn't he say so? How would he get there?"

"He could go on the bus," I said. "Maybe he went to get new eyeglasses. He buys his eyeglasses in the five-and-ten. He likes five-and-tens."

"He hates buses. He says they smell and they lurch."

I laughed. "He says they stink and they lurch in such a way

they churn the contents of your belly upside down." She
made no comment, so I said again, "He buys his glasses in
the five-and-ten in Buffalo and — "

"What?" she said. "I don't believe it."

"It's true. You ask Mother. She said that the last time they
went to Buffalo . . ." I tried to remember how long ago that
would have been.

"Well?"

"Well, Mother said she wanted to get a new hat and he
said that he'd be in the five-and-ten, and there was Samuel
and an old black man with him, and they were bent practically double over a counter. She told me, 'Your father had a
piece of newspaper in his hand and he had on a pair of
glasses, and he was looking at this newspaper, saying, "No,
not strong enough," and he moved on and picked up another
pair of glasses and put them on and said, "Let's see. Ah!
Fine!" Then he turned to this old black man, a dreadful-
looking old man, ragged and dirty and unshaven and
smelling foully of whiskey, and he said to him, "You got
yours?"' Mother said, 'Samuel, whatever are you doing?'
Even when she told it, she sounded horrified. He said, 'I'm
getting my glasses.' Then he asked the old man if he'd got
his, and the old man nodded and looked at Mother and sort
of slunk away. I suppose she had on one of those flowered
hats and white gloves. Mother said she looked at the counter
and there were rows and rows of glasses and they were all
fifty cents apiece. And that's what Samuel uses — that's what
he's always used. He says that he doesn't need special lenses,
that he hasn't anything unusual the matter with his eyes. All
he needs is some magnifying glass so that he can see to read
small printed matter, and so that's why he buys his glasses
in the five-and-ten." I stopped talking.

My aunt didn't say anything. She frowned at me.

So I started again. "He gets two pair at a time. Sometimes
he loses them. Sometimes he breaks them. You know he likes

to push them up high on top of his forehead, out of the way when he isn't using them, and his bald head is always greasy or sweaty and the glasses slide off on the floor and quite often they break. Didn't you know that?"

She said, "No, and I wish you'd stop calling your father Samuel." She went to wait on a customer.

I sat down on the high stool in front of the prescription counter. I didn't believe that my father had gone to Buffalo. He wouldn't go away without leaving any message. I wondered if he'd been kidnapped, and dismissed the idea as ridiculous. Something must have happened to him.

My mother called the store again, and right afterward Aunt Sophronia told Pedro to go in through the kitchen door and get coffee and sandwiches that Mrs. Layen had made and bring them into the store. We ate in the back room, one at a time. We didn't eat very much. I didn't like the smell of the coffee. It has always seemed to me that the human liver doesn't like coffee, that it makes the liver shiver. But all my family drank coffee and so did Pedro, and they didn't like to have me tell them how I felt about it.

I sat in the back room with that liver-shivering smell in my nose and looked out the back door. It was a pleasant place to sit and eat. It was a big room, and the rafters in the ceiling were exposed. True, there was a lot of clutter — pots and pans and mops and brooms, and big copper kettles stuck in corners or hanging from the rafters, and piles of old newspapers and magazines stacked on empty cartons. The walls were lined with small boxes that contained herbs. Some wholesale druggist had thrown them out, and my father had said he'd take them, because a dried herb would be good a hundred years from now; if it were properly dried, it would not lose its special properties. The back room always smelled faintly of aromatic substances — a kind of sneeze-making smell. The door was open, and I could look out into the back yard and see the cherry trees and the forsythia and all the flowering shrubs and the tender new grass.

We were very busy in the store all that afternoon. At five o'clock, my mother came in through the back door and sat down in the prescription room. She kept looking out of the window, toward the green. She had on a hat — a dark blue straw hat with small white flowers across the front — and her best black summer suit and white gloves. She was obviously dressed for an emergency, for disaster, prepared to identify Samuel Layen in hospital or morgue or police station.

The customers came in a steady stream. They bought the afternoon papers, cigarettes, tobacco. Men on their way home from work stopped to get ice cream for dessert. As the afternoon wore along, the shadows from the elm trees lengthened until they were as long as the green was wide. The iron urn in the middle looked chalk white. As the daylight slowly diminished, the trunks of the trees — that great expanse of trunk without branches, characteristic of the elms — seemed to be darkening and darkening.

I turned on the lights in the store and the student lamp on the prescription counter. It wasn't really quite dark enough to justify turning on the lights and I thought my aunt would say this, but she didn't. She asked my mother if she would like a glass of ginger ale.

"That would be very nice, thank you," my mother said. Her voice was deeper and harsher, and its carrying quality seemed to have increased.

"Pedro, get Mrs. Layen a glass of ginger ale."

When Pedro brought the ginger ale, Mother took a sip of it and then put it on the windowsill. It stayed there — bubbles forming, breaking, breaking, forming, breaking, until finally it was just a glass of yellowish liquid sitting forgotten on the windowsill.

When there weren't any customers in the store, we all went into the prescription room and sat down and waited with my mother. We sat in silence — Pedro and Aunt Sophronia and my mother and I. I kept thinking, But my father wouldn't leave us of his own free will. Only this morning at breakfast he said he wouldn't want to live anywhere else in the world except right here where we live. It could be suicide, or he could have been murdered. Certainly not kidnapped for ransom. What do we own? We don't own a car. There's the old building where we live and there's the store with its ancient mahogany-colored fixtures and glass-enclosed cases and the fountain room. But if it were all put together with our clothes and our household goods — pots and pans and chairs and tables and sofas and beds and mirrors — it wouldn't add up to anything to kidnap a man for.

Then I thought, Perhaps he left my mother for another woman. Preposterous. He was always saying that the first time he saw her she was sixteen and he decided right then and there he was going to marry her; she had big, black, snappy eyes, and her skin was so brown and so beautiful. His friends said he would be robbing the cradle, because he was twenty-four. He did marry her when she was eighteen. He said that whenever he looked at her he always thought, Black is the color of my true love's hair.

Aunt Sophronia said, "Perhaps we should put something in the newspaper — something . . ."

My mother said, "No," harshly. "The Layens would descend like a horde of locusts, crying, 'Samuel! Samuel! Samuel!' No. They all read the Buffalo *Recorder* and they would be down from Buffalo before we could turn around twice. Sometimes I think they use some form of astral projection. No. We won't put anything in the newspapers, not even if . . ."

I knew she was going to say, or had stopped herself from saying, "even if he is dead," though I did not see how she could keep an account of his death out of the newspapers.

My mother said my father's family was like a separate and

warlike tribe — arrogant, wary, hostile. She thought they were probably descended from the Watusi. In Buffalo, they moved through the streets in groups of three or four. She always had the impression they were stalking something. Their voices were very low in pitch, almost guttural, and unless you listened closely you got the impression they were not speaking English but were simply making an accented sound — uh-uh-uh-*uh* — that only they could understand.

Whenever my great-grandfather, the bearded patriarch of the family, went out on the streets of Buffalo, he was accompanied by one of his grandsons, a boy about fourteen, tall, quick-moving. The boy was always given the same instructions: "Anything happen to your grandfather, anybody say anything to him, you come straight back here, straight back here." "Anybody say anything to him" meant if anyone called him "out of his name." If this occurred, my mother said the boy would go straight home with the old man and emerge in the company of Uncle Joe, Uncle Bill, Uncle Bobby, Uncle John, Uncle George, my father, Aunt Kate, and Aunt Hal — all of them hellbent on vengeance.

They had lived in New Jersey — they always said "Jersey" — at the foot of a mountain they called Sour Mountain. When they first came to New York State, they lived in Albany. The whole clan — Great-Grandma, Great-Grandpa, Grandma and Grandpa, and all eight children including my father, Samuel, and a baby — came to Albany on one of the Hudson River boats. They had six ducks in wooden cages going splat all over the deck, a huge, woolly black dog — ancestry unknown, temper vicious — and six painted parlor chairs that Great-Grandma insisted on bringing with her. The men and boys wore black felt hats, and the skin on their faces and hands was almost as dark as the felt of the hats. They wore heavy black suits that Great-Grandma had made for them. Whenever anyone approached them on the boat, they executed a kind of flanking motion and very quickly formed a circle, the men facing the outside, the women on the inside.

My mother once told me she knew all the details about the arrival of these black strangers in Albany, because her family had known a black man who worked on the Hudson River boats and he had told her father about it. When the boat approached the dock, it had to be maneuvered into position, and so it started to move back down the river. It did not go very far, but there was an ever-increasing length of water between the boat and the dock. The sun was out, the brass railings gleamed in the sunlight, and the white paint sparkled as the boat edged away from the dock. The dark-skinned, fierce-looking men held a conference. The old bearded man who was my great-grandfather gave a cry — a trumpeting kind of cry — and took a long running leap off the boat and landed on the dock, hitting it with his cane and bellowing, "You ain't takin' us back now, you know! Throw that baby down to me! Throw that baby down to me!" There were outraged cries from the people on the deck. One of the Layens threw the baby down to the old man and he caught it. He glared up at the scowling deckhands and the staring people and shouted, "Ain't goin' to take us back now, you know! We paid to get here. Ain't going to take us back now. Jump!" he roared. "All of you, jump!"

My mother said the black man told her father this story, and he ended it by saying, "You know, those people jumped off that boat — even the women. They picked up all their stuff, even those damn ducks and that vicious dog and those chairs, and they took these long running leaps and landed on the dock. I never saw anything like it. And that old bearded black man kept walking up and down on the dock, hitting it with his cane, and he's got this baby, dangling it by one foot, and he's hollering out and hollering out, 'We paid to get here! Ain't goin' to take us back now, you know!'"

I sat in the prescription room staring at my mother and

thinking again, If my father died, she would not tell his
family? Even if he died? She would be afraid to tell them for
fear they would arrive in Wheeling and attack all the
inhabitants — they would be as devastating as a gang of
professional stranglers. Old as he was now, my great-
grandfather wouldn't ride in an automobile and he didn't
like trains, so he would probably walk down to Wheeling
from Buffalo, muttering to himself, intractable, dangerous,
his beard quivering with rage, his little eyes blazing with the
light of battle.

Customers kept coming into the store. Pedro and I waited
on them. Once, when we were both behind the tobacco
counter, he said, "I could just walk around in the town and
look for him. I wouldn't tell people he was lost."

I shook my head. "Aunt Sophronia wouldn't like it."

Each time the phone rang, I answered it. I left the door of
the phone booth open, so they could all hear what I said, in
case it was some kind of news about my father. It never was.
It was always somebody who wanted some of his chocolate
syrup, or his special-formula cold cream, or his lotion for
acne. I kept saying the same thing in reply. "He isn't here
right now. We expect him, we expect him. When? Later. We
expect him later."

There was an automatic closing device on the screen door
which kept it from banging shut. It made a hissing sound
when the door was opened. Each time we heard that hiss, we
all looked toward the door expectantly, thinking perhaps
this time it would be Samuel. Finally, Aunt Sophronia turned
on a small radio on the prescription counter. There was a
great deal of static, voices came in faintly, and there was a
thin thread of music in the background — a confusion of
sounds. I had never known my aunt to turn on the radio in
the store. My father said that only certain kinds of decaying
drugstores had radios blatting in them, and that the owners
turned them on hoping to distract the customers' attention

away from the leaks in the roof, the holes in the floor, the
flyblown packages, and the smell of cat.

Aunt Sophronia sat on the high stool in front of the
prescription counter, bent forward a little, listening. We all
listened. My mother looked down at her hands, Pedro looked
at the floor, Aunt Sophronia looked at the black and white
linoleum on the counter. I thought, We're waiting to hear
one of those fudge-voiced announcers say that a short thick-
bodied black man has been found on the railroad track, train
gone over him, or he's been found hanging or shot or
drowned. Why drowned? Well, the river's close by.

I practiced different versions of the story. "Young woman
finds short, thick-bodied, unidentified black man." "School
children find colored druggist in river." "Negro pharmacist
lost in mountains." "Black man shot by white man in love
duel." Colored druggist. Negro pharmacist. Black man. My
father? I hovered in the doorway listening to the radio —
world news roundup, weather, terrible music. Nothing
about unidentified black men.

Aunt Sophronia turned toward my mother and said
something in a low voice.

"Police?" my mother said in a very loud voice, and
repeated it. "Police?"

"He's been gone since nine o'clock this morning. What
else can we do except call the police?"

"No!" My mother's voice was louder and harsher than I
had ever heard it. "There's no need to go to the police. We
don't know where Samuel is, but if we wait patiently we'll
find out." Her eyes were open very wide and they glistened.
It occurred to me that they might be luminous in the dark,
like a cat's eyes.

"He might have had an accident."

"We would have been informed," my mother said firmly.
"His name is engraved on the inside of his watch. His name
is on his shirt and on his underwear and his handkerchiefs.

I mark everything with indelible ink."

"But if it happened in Buffalo — "

"If what happened? What are you talking about?"

Aunt Sophronia began to cry. Right there in the prescription room. She made so much noise you could hear her out in the store. I was appalled. The private part of our life had suddenly and noisily entered the public part — or perhaps it was the other way around. When people cry and try to talk at the same time, their words come out jerkily and they have to speak between the taking of big convulsive breaths, and so they cannot control the volume of their speech and they shout, and that is what my quiet-voiced Aunt Sophronia was doing. She was shouting right there in the drugstore. Someone came into the store and turned to look toward the prescription room to see what was going on. Pedro ran out of the room to wait on the customer.

"I'm just as fond of him as you are!" Aunt Sophronia shouted between sobs and gasps and agonized-sounding crying noises. "Just as worried as you are! You can't just sit there and let him disappear! And not do anything about it!"

My mother stood up, looked at me, and said, "Call a taxi." Then she turned to my aunt and said, "We will go to the Tenyeck Barracks and discuss this with the state police." Her voice was pitched so low and it was so loud that it sounded like a man's voice.

When the town taxi came, I stood in the doorway and watched them go down the front steps. It was perfectly obvious that my aunt had been crying, for her eyelids were red and swollen. My mother looked ill. They both seemed to have shrunk in size. They were bent over and so looked smaller and shorter than they actually were. When they reached the sidewalk, they turned and glanced up at me. I felt like crying, too. The flowered hat had slipped so far back on my mother's head that it made her look as though she were bald. Aunt Sophronia had a yellow pencil stuck in her hair, and she had put on an old black coat that hung in the back room. The coat was too big for her; the sleeves were too long and it reached almost to her ankles. Under it, she was still wearing the gray cotton store coat. They looked like little old women — humble, questing, moving slowly. When they turned, I could see the white part of their eyes under the irises, and I had to look away from them.

Aunt Sophronia said, "If there are any prescriptions, I'll fill them later." Then she took my mother by the arm and they went toward the taxi. The driver got out and held the door open for them and closed it behind them.

I wondered what my mother would say to the state police. "My husband is missing. He is a short, broad-shouldered black man, bald-headed, forty-eight years old"? Would the state police snicker and say, "Yes, we would hardly expect you, with your dark brown skin, to be married to a white man. Wearing what when last seen?" "Light gray summer suit and polka-dot bow tie, highly polished black shoes." The gravel path that bisects the village green was very dry this morning — no mud. So there would still have been polish on his shoes. But not if he were drowned. But who would drown him, and why? Might have drowned himself. Drowned himself? Surely she will say that he has only three teeth, three teeth only — one in the upper jaw and two in the lower jaw.

Then I thought, But why did they have to go to the police? Why couldn't they have telephoned? Because someone might have overheard the conversation. So what difference would that make? Did they think the police would send out a silent and invisible bloodhound to hunt for the black druggist from Wheeling? Did they think the police would send out invisible men to search the morgues in Buffalo, to fish for a fresh black corpse in the streams and coves and brooks in and around Wheeling?

We didn't even hunt for him the way white people would

have hunted for their father. It was all indirect. Has he been
to the post office? . . . "Oh, oh, oh." Has he been to the
railroad station to pick up an express package? . . . "I see, I
see, I see."

Between customers I thought, We've even infected Pedro,
who is Portuguese, with this disease, whatever it is. Why did
we have to hunt for my father this way? Because there is
something scandalous about a disappearance, especially if it
is a black man who disappears. Could be caused by a
shortage of funds (What funds? His own?), a shortage of
narcotics, unpaid bills, a mistake made in a prescription —
scandal, scandal, scandal. Black druggist, mixed up with
police, disappears. Mixed up with police.

It wasn't until Miss Rena Randolph handed me an empty
prescription bottle to be refilled that I realized what my aunt
had done. I held the sticky bottle in my hand, the label all
over gravy drips, as my father was wont to say, and I
thought, Why, I'm in charge of the drugstore and I am only
fifteen. The only other person working in the store is Pedro,
and he is only twelve. All my life I'd heard conversations
about "uncovered" drugstores — drugstores without a
pharmacist on the premises. For the first time, our store was
"uncovered." Suppose something happened . . .

Miss Randolph leaned against the counter and coughed
and coughed and coughed. "I won't need it until morning,"
she said, pointing at the bottle that I held. "I have more at
home. I always keep two bottles ahead."

My father told me once that he thought she looked as
though she had just been dug up out of her grave. She was
a very unhealthy-looking old woman. She was tall and very
thin. Her skin was gray, her clothes were gray, and her hair
was gray. But her teeth were yellow. She wore eyeglasses
with no rims. Just last week when my father was refilling this
same prescription for her, he said, "I don't know what Doc
keeps giving her this stuff for. Perfectly obvious what's the

matter with her, and this isn't going to cure it."

"What *is* the matter with her?" I asked.

He shrugged his shoulders and said evasively, "Your guess is just as good as mine — or Doc's."

"I can get it in the morning," she repeated now.

"Yes, ma'am. It will be ready in the morning."

"Quiet in here tonight. Where's your aunt?"

"Outside," I said, and the way I said it made it sound as though I meant "transported" or "sold down the river."

She looked around the store as though she were a stranger, seeing it for the first time. She said, "It's a nice night. I suppose she's working in the garden."

After Miss Randolph left, I looked around the store, too. What had she seen that made her say it was a nice night and that my aunt would be working in the garden? You couldn't really see what was on the shelves — just the gleam of bottles and jars inside the dark-mahogany, glass-enclosed cases. The corners lay in deep shadow. It might have been a conjurer's shop, except, of course, for the cigarettes and the candy and the soda fountain. The bottles gleaming darkly along the walls could have held wool of bat and nose of Turk, root of the mandrake and dust of the toad. I went out in the back room and looked into the yard. It seemed to go on forever, reaching into a vast, mysterious distance, unexplored, silent — not even the twitter of a bird. It was pitch black. I couldn't see the blossoms on the cherry trees, I couldn't tell what shape the yard was. But I now knew what was wrong with Miss Rena Randolph. She was crazy.

As the evening wore along, we got fewer and fewer customers. They bought cigarettes and cigars, candy, magazines. Very few cars went past. The town clock struck nine, and this surprised me, because I hadn't realized it was so late. My father always closed the store at nine-thirty. I had never closed it — or opened it, for that matter. I did not know where the keys to the front door were kept. I watched the clock, wondering what I should do at nine-thirty.

At quarter past nine, there was only one customer in the store — a woman who had purchased a box of candy. I was wrapping it up for her when someone pulled the screen door open with an abrupt, yanking movement and Pedro said, "Ah — "

I looked up and saw my father standing in the doorway, swaying back and forth, his arms extended. As I watched, he reached out and supported himself by leaning against the doorjamb. His appearance was so strange, he seemed so weak, so unlike himself, that I thought, He's been wounded. I peered at him, hunting for bruises on his face or his hands. As he entered the store, he kept looking around, blinking. He was wearing his light gray suit, and his newest boater hat, and the bow tie that I remembered. But the tie was twisted around to one side and it was partly untied, and his suit looked rumpled and so did his shirt.

I escorted the customer to the door, held it open for her, and then went to my father and said, "We — we didn't know where you were. Are you all right?"

He patted my hand. He said, "Look," and he smiled, revealing a set of glittering, horrible, wolfish-looking false teeth. There was a dribble of dried blood at the corner of his mouth. "I got my teeth."

I could barely understand what he said. He sounded as though he were speaking through or around a formidable obstruction that prevented his tongue and his lips from performing their normal function. The teeth glistened like the white porcelain fixtures in the downstairs bathroom.

I said, "Oh," weakly.

Pedro patted my father's arm. He said, "I worried — "

"Am I always going to sound like this?"

"I don't think so," I said.

He went into the prescription room and sat down in the

chair by the window. Pedro stood beside him. I sat down on
the high stool in front of the counter.

"Where's Sophy?"

I jumped off the stool. "They've gone to the police. I must
telephone them — "

"Police? Police?" He made whistling noises when he said
this. "Jesus Christ! For what?"

"They thought you were lost. I've got to call the Barracks — "

"Lawth?" he said, angrily. "Loweth?" he roared. "Lowerth? How could I we lowerth?" He stopped talking, reached
up and took out the new false teeth, and wrapped them
in his handkerchief. When he spoke again, he sounded just
like himself. "I read about this place in Norwich where they
take all your teeth out at once and put the false teeth in—
make them for you and put them in all the same day. That's
where I was. In Norwich. Getting my teeth. How could I get
lost?"

"Oh!" I said and put my hand over my mouth, keeping
the pain away. "Didn't it hurt? Don't the teeth hurt?"

"Hurt?" he shouted. "Of course they hurt!"

"But why didn't you tell Mother you were going!"

"I didn't think I'd be gone more than two hours. I got on
a bus up at the corner, and it didn't take long to get there.
They pulled the teeth out. Then they took impressions. They
wouldn't let me have the teeth right away, said they had to
wait to make sure the jaw had stopped bleeding, and so the
whole process took longer than I thought it would."

"What made you finally get false teeth?" I didn't think it
was pictures of the Valentino types, with their perfect white
teeth, that I'd left around for him to see, and I didn't think
it was the sight of Gramps Fender, the old man who took
care of the house next door and whose false teeth hung loose
in his mouth, or the fact that my Aunt Sophronia and my
mother kept talking about the importance of chewing as an

aid to the digestion of food. So if it wasn't any of these things, then what was it?

He sighed and said that that morning, while he was shaving, he had run through a solo he was to sing in church on Sunday. He stood in front of that new plate-glass mirror in the downstairs bathroom under all that brilliant white light, and he opened his mouth wide, and he saw himself in the mirror — the open mouth all red and moist inside, and the naked gums with a tooth here and there, and it was the mouth of an idiot out of Shakespeare, it was the mouth of the nurse in *Romeo and Juliet*, the mouth of the gravediggers in Hamlet, but most shocking of all, it was the mouth of Samuel Layen. This was what the congregation looked at and into on Sunday mornings. He said he couldn't bear the thought that that was what all those white people saw when he sang a solo. If he hadn't seen his mouth wide open like that in the new mirror under that new light . . .

I thought, But the congregation couldn't possibly see the inside of his mouth — he's in the choir loft when he sings, and he's much too far away from them. But I didn't say this.

He said it was while he was standing under the first cherry tree, looking up at the sky and listening to the hum of the bees, that he decided he would take a bus and head for Norwich and get himself some false teeth that very day without saying anything about it to anyone. He put the teeth back in his mouth and turned to Pedro and said, in that mumbling, full-of-pebbles voice, "How do I look?" and he smiled.

Pedro said, "You look beautiful, Mr. Layen," and touched him gently on the shoulder.

I went into the phone booth and closed the door. I started to dial the number of the state police. It was on a card up over the phone, along with the telephone numbers of the local doctors and the firehouse. I hesitated. The phone booth smelled of all its recent users — of cigar smoke, perfume, sweat. I felt as constrained as though all of these people were in the booth with me: politicians, idle females, workmen. I couldn't imagine myself saying, "We thought my father was missing. He's been gone all day and my mother and my aunt have now reported him as missing, but he's back." Why didn't I feel free to say this? Was it the presence of those recent users of the phone booth, who might ask, "Where'd he go?" "Has he done this before?" "Has he got a girl friend?" I dialed the number, and a gruff voice said, "State Police. Tenyeck Barracks. Officer O'Toole speaking."

I didn't know what to say to him, so I didn't say anything.

The voice sounded loud, impatient, in my ear. "*Hu*llo! *He*llo? Speak up! Speak up!"

If I said that we thought my father was missing but he isn't, he's found, he's back, then wouldn't this Officer O'Toole want to know where he'd been? I said, "Well —"

The voice said, "Hello? Hello?" and "Yes?" and "What is it?" It was a very gruff voice and it had a barking quality.

I shook my head at the voice. I was not free to speak openly to that gruff policeman's voice. I thought, Well, now, perhaps the reason my father hadn't wanted to replace his teeth was that one of the images of the black man that the white man carries around with him is of white teeth flashing in a black and grinning face. So my father went toothless to destroy that image. But then there is toothless old Uncle Tom, and my old black mammy with her head rag is toothless, too, and without teeth my father fitted *that* image of the black man, didn't he?

So he was damned either way. Was he not? And so was I. And so was I.

Then I thought, Why bother? Why not act just like other people, just this once, just like white people — come right out and say the lost is found. My hand, my own hand, had in response to some order from my subconscious reached for a pencil that was securely fastened to a nail in the booth, tied

there by a long red string. The pencil hung next to a big
white pad. This was where we wrote down telephone orders.
I was doodling on the big white pad. The skin on my hand
was so dark in contrast to the white pad that I stared, because
that was the second time that day that I had taken a good
look at the color of my skin against something stark white.
I looked at my dark brown hand and thought, Throw that
baby down to me, you ain't goin' to take us back now, you
know; all of us people with this dark skin must help hold the
black island inviolate. I said, "This is Mr. Layen's daughter,
at Layen's Drugstore in Wheeling. Mrs. Layen and her sister,
Miss Bart, are on their way over there. Will you tell them
that Mr. Layen found his watch — "

"Found his watch? He lost it, did he? Valuable watch, I
suppose. Wait a minute. They're just coming up the steps
now, just coming in the door. Wait a minute. I'll let you talk
to Mrs. Layen yourself."

Everybody knew us for miles around. We were those rare
laboratory specimens the black people who ran the drugstore
in the white town of Wheeling, New York, only black family
in town except for the Granites, who, ha, ha, ha —

"Wait a minute," the gruff, barking voice said again.

I closed my eyes and I could see my mother and my aunt —
two bent-over little women, going up the steps of the state-
police barracks in Tenyeck, humble, hesitant, the whites of
their eyes showing under the irises.

My mother's voice sounded in my ear. "Yes?" Harsh, loud.

I said, "Father is so happy. He found his watch. He thinks
he dropped it in Norwich, where he went to get his new false
teeth." It sounded as though he'd always had false teeth — or
at least Officer O'Toole, who was undoubtedly listening in,
would think so.

A VISIT OF CHARITY

Eudora Welty

It was mid-morning — a very cold, bright day. Holding a potted plant before her, a girl of 14 jumped off the bus in front of the Old Ladies' Home, on the outskirts of town. She wore a red coat, and her straight yellow hair was hanging down loose from the pointed white cap all the little girls were wearing that year. She stopped for a moment beside one of the prickly dark shrubs with which the city had beautified the Home, and then proceeded slowly toward the building, which was of whitewashed brick and reflected the winter sunlight like a block of ice. As she walked vaguely up the steps she shifted the small pot from hand to hand; then she had to set it down and remove her mittens before she could open the heavy door.

"I'm a Campfire Girl. . . . I have to pay a visit to some old lady," she told the nurse at the desk. This was a woman in a white uniform who looked as if she were cold; she had close-cut hair which stood up on the very top of her head exactly like a sea wave. Marian, the little girl, did not tell her that this visit would give her a minimum of only three points in her score.

"Acquainted with any of our residents?" asked the nurse. She lifted one eyebrow and spoke like a man.

"With any old ladies? No — but — that is, any of them will do," Marian stammered. With her free hand she pushed her hair behind her ears, as she did when it was time to study Science.

The nurse shrugged and rose, "You have a nice *multiflora cineraria* there," she remarked as she walked ahead down the hall of closed doors to pick out an old lady.

There was loose, bulging linoleum on the floor. Marian

felt as if she were walking on the waves, but the nurse paid
no attention to it. There was a smell in the hall like the
interior of a clock. Everything was silent until, behind one of
the doors, an old lady of some kind cleared her throat like a
sheep bleating. This decided the nurse. Stopping in her tracks,
she first extended her arm, bent her elbow, and leaned
forward from the hips — all to examine the watch strapped
to her wrist; then she gave a loud double-rap on the door.

"There are two in each room," the nurse remarked over
her shoulder.

"Two what?" asked Marian without thinking. The sound
like sheep's bleating almost made her turn around and run
back.

One old woman was pulling the door open in short,
gradual jerks, and when she saw the nurse a strange smile
forced her old face dangerously awry. Marian, suddenly
propelled by the strong, impatient arm of the nurse, saw next
the side-face of another old woman, even older, who was
lying flat in bed with a cap on and a counterpane drawn up
to her chin.

"Visitor," said the nurse, and after one more shove she
was off up the hall.

Marian stood tongue-tied; both hands held the potted
plant. The old woman, still with that terrible, square smile
(which was a smile of welcome) stamped on her bony face,
was waiting. . . . Perhaps she said something. The old woman
in bed said nothing at all, and she did not look around.

Suddenly Marian saw a hand, quick as a bird claw, reach
up in the air and pluck the white cap off her head. At
the same time, another claw to match drew her all the way
into the room, and the next moment the door closed behind
her.

"My, my, my," said the old lady at her side.

Marian stood enclosed by a bed, a washstand and a chair;
the tiny room had altogether too much furniture. Everything

smelled wet — even the bare floor. She held onto the back of the chair, which was wicker and felt soft and damp. Her heart beat more and more slowly, her hands got colder and colder, and she could not hear whether the old women were saying anything or not. She could not see them very clearly. How dark it was! The window shade was down, and the only door was shut. Marian looked at the ceiling. . . . It was like being caught in a robber's cave, just before one was murdered.

"Did you come to be our little girl for a while?" the first robber asked.

Then something was snatched from Marian's hand — the little potted plant.

"Flowers!" screamed the old woman. She stood holding the pot in an undecided way. "Pretty flowers," she added.

Then the old woman in bed cleared her throat and spoke. "They are not pretty," she said, still without looking around, but very distinctly.

Marian suddenly pitched against the chair and sat down in it.

"Pretty flowers," the first old woman insisted. "Pretty — pretty . . ."

Marian wished she had the little pot back for just a moment — she had forgotten to look at the plant herself before giving it away. What did it look like?

"Stinkweeds," said the other old woman sharply. She had a bunchy white forehead and red eyes like a sheep. Now she turned them toward Marian. The fogginess seemed to rise in her throat again, and she bleated, "Who — are — you?"

To her surprise, Marian could not remember her name. "I'm a Campfire Girl," she said finally.

"Watch out for the germs," said the old woman like a sheep, not addressing anyone.

"One came out last month to see us," said the first old woman.

A sheep or a germ? wondered Marian dreamily, holding onto the chair.

"Did not!" cried the other old woman.

"Did so! Read to us out of the Bible, and we enjoyed it!" screamed the first.

"Who enjoyed it?" said the woman in bed. Her mouth was unexpectedly small and sorrowful, like a pet's.

"We enjoyed it," insisted the other. "You enjoyed it, I enjoyed it."

"We all enjoyed it," said Marian, without realizing that she had said a word.

The first old woman had just finished putting the potted plant high, high on the top of the wardrobe, where it could hardly be seen from below. Marian wondered how she had ever succeeded in placing it there, how she could ever have reached so high.

"You mustn't pay any attention to old Addie," she now said to the little girl. "She's ailing today."

"Will you shut your mouth?" said the old woman in bed. "I am not."

"You're a story."

"I can't stay but a minute — really, I can't," said Marian suddenly. She looked down at the wet floor and thought that if she were sick in here they would have to let her go.

With much to-do the first old woman sat down in a rocking chair — still another piece of furniture! — and began to rock. With the fingers of one hand she touched a very dirty cameo pin on her chest. "What do you do at school?" she asked.

"I don't know. . . ." said Marian. She tried to think but she could not.

"Oh, but the flowers are beautiful," the old woman whispered. She seemed to rock faster and faster; Marian did not see how anyone could rock so fast.

"Ugly," said the woman in bed.

"If we bring flowers — " Marian began, and then fell silent. She had almost said that if Campfire Girls brought flowers to the Old Ladies' Home, the visit would count one extra point and if they took a Bible with them on the bus and read it to the old ladies, it counted double. But the old woman had not listened, anyway; she was rocking and watching the other one, who watched back from the bed.

"Poor Addie is ailing. She has to take medicine — see?" she said, pointing a horny finger at a row of bottles on the table, and rocking so high that her black comfort shoes lifted off the floor like a little child's.

"I am no more sick than you are," said the woman in bed.

"Oh, yes you are!"

"I just got more sense than you have, that's all," said the other old woman, nodding her head.

"That's only the contrary way she talks when *you all* come," said the first old lady with sudden intimacy. She stopped the rocker with a neat pat of her feet and leaned toward Marian. Her hand reached over — it felt like a petunia leaf, clinging and just a little sticky.

"Will you hush! Will you hush!" cried the other one.

Marian leaned back rigidly in her chair.

"When I was a little girl like you, I went to school and all," said the old woman in the same intimate, menacing voice. "Not here — another town . . ."

"Hush!" said the sick woman. "You never went to school. You never came and you never went. You never were anything — only here. You never were born! You don't know anything. Your head is empty, your heart and hands and your old black purse are all empty, even that little old box that you brought with you you brought empty — you showed it to me. And yet you talk, talk, talk, talk, talk all the time until I think I'm losing my mind! Who are you? You're a stranger — a perfect stranger! Don't you know you're a stranger? Is it possible that they have actually done a thing like this to anyone — sent them in a stranger to talk, and rock, and tell away her whole long rigmarole? Do they seriously suppose that I'll be able to keep it up, day in, day out, night in, night out, living in the same room with a terrible old woman — forever?"

Marian saw the old woman's eyes grow bright and turn toward her. This old woman was looking at her with despair and calculation in her face. Her small lips suddenly dropped apart, and exposed a half circle of false teeth with tan gum.

"Come here, I want to tell you something," she whispered. "Come here!"

Marian was trembling, and her heart nearly stopped beating altogether for a moment.

"Now, now, Addie," said the first old woman. "That's not polite. Do you know what's really the matter with old Addie today?" She too looked at Marian; one of her eyelids drooped low.

"The matter?" the child repeated stupidly. "What's the matter with her?"

"Why, she's mad because it's her birthday!" said the first old woman, beginning to rock again and giving a little crow as though she had answered her own riddle.

"It is not, it is not!" screamed the old woman in bed. "It is not my birthday, no one knows when that is but myself, and will you please be quiet and say nothing more, or I'll go straight out of my mind!" She turned her eyes toward Marian again, and presently she said in the soft, foggy voice, "When the worst comes to the worst, I ring this bell, and the nurse comes." One of her hands was drawn out from under the patched counterpane — a thin little hand with enormous black freckles. With a finger which would not hold still she pointed to a little bell on the table among the bottles.

"How old are you?" Marian breathed. Now she could see the old woman in bed very closely and plainly, and very abruptly, from all sides, as in dreams. She wondered about her — she wondered for a moment as though there was nothing else in the world to wonder about. It was the first time such a thing had happened to Marian.

"I won't tell!"

The old face on the pillow, where Marian was bending over it, slowly gathered and collapsed. Soft whimpers came out of the small open mouth. It was a sheep that she sounded like — a little lamb. Marian's face drew very close, the yellow hair hung forward.

"She's crying!" She turned a bright, burning face up to the first old woman.

"That's Addie for you," the old woman said spitefully.

Marian jumped up and moved toward the door. For the second time, the claw almost touched her hair, but it was not quick enough. The little girl put her cap on.

"Well, it was a real visit," said the old woman, following Marian through the doorway and all the way out into the hall. Then from behind she suddenly clutched the child with her sharp little fingers. In an affected, high-pitched whine she cried, "Oh, little girl, have you a penny to spare for a poor old woman that's not got anything of her own? We don't have a thing in the world — not a penny for candy — not a thing! Little girl, just a nickel — a penny — "

Marian pulled violently against the old hands for a moment before she was free. Then she ran down the hall, without looking behind her and without looking at the nurse who was reading *Field & Stream* at her desk. The nurse, after another triple motion to consult her wristwatch, asked automatically the question put to visitors in all institutions: "Won't you stay and have dinner with *us*?"

Marian never replied. She pushed the heavy door open into the cold air and ran down the steps.

Under the prickly shrub she stooped and quickly, without being seen, retrieved a red apple she had hidden there.

Her yellow hair under the white cap, her scarlet coat, her

bare knees all flashed in the sunlight as she ran to meet the big bus rocketing through the street.

"Wait for me!" she shouted. As though at an imperial command, the bus ground to a stop.

She jumped on and took a big bite out of the apple.

NEIGHBOUR ROSICKY

Willa Cather

I

When Doctor Burleigh told neighbour Rosicky he had a bad heart, Rosicky protested.

"So? No, I guess my heart was always pretty good. I got a little asthma, maybe. Just a awful short breath when I was pitchin' hay last summer, dat's all."

"Well now, Rosicky, if you know more about it than I do, what did you come to me for? It's your heart that makes you short of breath, I tell you. You're sixty-five years old, and you've always worked hard, and your heart's tired. You've got to be careful from now on, and you can't do heavy work any more. You've got five boys at home to do it for you."

The old farmer looked up at the Doctor with a gleam of amusement in his queer triangular-shaped eyes. His eyes were large and lively, but the lids were caught up in the middle in a curious way, so that they formed a triangle. He did not look like a sick man. His brown face was creased but not wrinkled, he had a ruddy colour in his smooth-shaven cheeks and in his lips, under his long brown moustache. His hair was thin and ragged around his ears, but very little grey. His forehead, naturally high and crossed by deep parallel lines, now ran all the way up to his pointed crown. Rosicky's face had the habit of looking interested, — suggested a contented disposition and a reflective quality that was gay rather than grave. This gave him a certain detachment, the easy manner of an onlooker and observer.

"Well, I guess you ain't got no pills fur a bad heart, Doctor Ed. I guess the only thing is fur me to git me a new one."

Doctor Burleigh swung round in his desk-chair and

frowned at the old farmer. "I think if I were you I'd take a
little care of the old one, Rosicky."

Rosicky shrugged. "Maybe I don't know how. I expect
you mean fur me not to drink my coffee no more."

"I wouldn't, in your place. But you'll do as you choose
about that. I've never yet been able to separate a Bohemian
from his coffee or his pipe. I've quit trying. But the sure thing
is you've got to cut out farm work. You can feed the stock
and do chores about the barn, but you can't do anything in
the fields that makes you short of breath."

"How about shelling corn?"

"Of course not!"

Rosicky considered with puckered brows.

"I can't make my heart go no longer'n it wants to, can I,
Doctor Ed?"

"I think it's good for five or six years yet, maybe more, if
you'll take the strain off it. Sit around the house and help
Mary. If I had a good wife like yours, I'd want to stay around
the house."

His patient chuckled. "It ain't no place fur a man. I don't
like no old man hanging round the kitchen too much. An'
my wife, she's a awful hard worker her own self."

"That's it; you can help her a little. My Lord, Rosicky, you
are one of the few men I know who has a family he can get
some comfort out of; happy dispositions, never quarrel
among themselves, and they treat you right. I want to see you
live a few years and enjoy them."

"Oh, they're good kids, all right," Rosicky assented.

The Doctor wrote him a prescription and asked him how
his oldest son, Rudolph, who had married in the spring, was
getting on. Rudolph had struck out for himself, on rented
land. "And how's Polly? I was afraid Mary mightn't like an
American daughter-in-law, but it seems to be working out all
right."

"Yes, she's a fine girl. Dat widder woman bring her

daughters up very nice. Polly got lots of spunk, an' she got some style, too. Da's nice, for young folks to have some style." Rosicky inclined his head gallantly. His voice and his twinkly smile were an affectionate compliment to his daughter-in-law.

"It looks like a storm, and you'd better be getting home before it comes. In town in the car?" Doctor Burleigh rose.

"No, I'm in de wagon. When you got five boys, you ain't got much chance to ride round in de Ford. I ain't much for cars, noway."

"Well, it's a good road out to your place; but I don't want you bumping around in a wagon much. And never again on a hay-rake, remember!"

Rosicky placed the Doctor's fee delicately behind the desk-telephone, looking the other way, as if this were an absent-minded gesture. He put on his plush cap and his corduroy jacket with a sheepskin collar, and went out.

The Doctor picked up his stethoscope and frowned at it as if he were seriously annoyed with the instrument. He wished it had been telling tales about some other man's heart, some old man who didn't look the Doctor in the eye so knowingly, or hold out such a warm brown hand when he said good-bye. Doctor Burleigh had been a poor boy in the country before he went away to medical school; he had known Rosicky almost ever since he could remember, and he had a deep affection for Mrs. Rosicky.

Only last winter he had had such a good breakfast at Rosicky's, and that when he needed it. He had been out all night on a long, hard confinement case at Tom Marshall's, — a big rich farm where there was plenty of stock and plenty of feed and a great deal of expensive farm machinery of the newest model, and no comfort whatever. The woman had too many children and too much work, and she was no manager. When the baby was born at last, and handed over to the assisting neighbour woman, and the mother was

properly attended to, Burleigh refused any breakfast in that
slovenly house, and drove his buggy — the snow was too
deep for a car — eight miles to Anton Rosicky's place. He
didn't know another farm-house where a man could get such
a warm welcome, and such good strong coffee with rich
cream. No wonder the old chap didn't want to give up his
coffee!

He had driven in just when the boys had come back from
the barn and were washing up for breakfast. The long table,
covered with a bright oilcloth, was set out with dishes
waiting for them, and the warm kitchen was full of the smell
of coffee and hot biscuit and sausage. Five big handsome
boys, running from twenty to twelve, all with what Burleigh
called natural good manners, — they hadn't a bit of the
painful self-consciousness he himself had to struggle with
when he was a lad. One ran to put his horse away, another
helped him off with his fur coat and hung it up, and
Josephine, the youngest child and the only daughter, quickly
set another place under her mother's direction.

With Mary, to feed creatures was the natural expression
of affection, — her chickens, the calves, her big hungry boys.
It was a rare pleasure to feed a young man whom she seldom
saw and of whom she was as proud as if he belonged to her.
Some country housekeepers would have stopped to spread a
white cloth over the oilcloth, to change the thick cups and
plates for their best china, and the wooden-handled knives
for plated ones. But not Mary.

"You must take us as you find us, Doctor Ed. I'd be glad
to put out my good things for you if you was expected, but
I'm glad to get you any way at all."

He knew she was glad, — she threw back her head and
spoke out as if she were announcing him to the whole prairie.
Rosicky hadn't said anything at all; he merely smiled his
twinkling smile, put some more coal on the fire, and went
into his own room to pour the Doctor a little drink in a

medicine glass. When they were all seated, he watched his wife's face from his end of the table and spoke to her in Czech. Then, with the instinct of politeness which seldom failed him, he turned to the Doctor and said slyly: "I was just tellin' her not to ask you no questions about Mrs. Marshall till you eat some breakfast. My wife, she's terrible fur to ask questions."

The boys laughed, and so did Mary. She watched the Doctor devour her biscuit and sausage, too much excited to eat anything herself. She drank her coffee and sat taking in everything about her visitor. She had known him when he was a poor country boy, and was boastfully proud of his success, always saying: "What do people go to Omaha for, to see a doctor, when we got the best one in the State right here?" If Mary liked people at all, she felt physical pleasure in the sight of them, personal exultation in any good fortune that came to them. Burleigh didn't know many women like that, but he knew she was like that.

When his hunger was satisfied, he did, of course, have to tell them about Mrs. Marshall, and he noticed what a friendly interest the boys took in the matter.

Rudolph, the oldest one (he was still living at home then), said: "The last time I was over there, she was lifting them big heavy milk-cans, and I knew she oughtn't to be doing it."

"Yes, Rudolph told me about that when he came home, and I said it wasn't right," Mary put in warmly. "It was all right for me to do them things up to the last, for I was terrible strong, but that woman's weakly. And do you think she'll be able to nurse it, Ed?" She sometimes forgot to give him the title she was so proud of. "And to think of your being up all night and then not able to get a decent breakfast! I don't know what's the matter with such people."

"Why, Mother," said one of the boys, "if Doctor Ed had got breakfast there, we wouldn't have him here. So you ought to be glad."

"He knows I'm glad to have him, John, any time. But I'm sorry for that poor woman, how bad she'll feel the Doctor had to go away in the cold without his breakfast."

"I wish I'd been in practice when these were getting born." The doctor looked down the row of close-clipped heads. "I missed some good breakfasts by not being."

The boys began to laugh at their mother because she flushed so red, but she stood her ground and threw up her head. "I don't care, you wouldn't have got away from this house without breakfast. No doctor ever did. I'd have had something ready fixed that Anton could warm up for you."

The boys laughed harder than ever, and exclaimed at her: "I'll bet you would!" "She would, that!"

"Father, did you get breakfast for the doctor when we were born?"

"Yes, and he used to bring me my breakfast, too, mighty nice. I was always awful hungry!" Mary admitted with a guilty laugh.

While the boys were getting the Doctor's horse, he went to the window to examine the house plants. "What do you do to your geraniums to keep them blooming all winter, Mary? I never pass this house that from the road I don't see your windows full of flowers."

She snapped off a dark red one, and a ruffled new green leaf, and put them in his buttonhole. "There, that looks better. You look too solemn for a young man, Ed. Why don't you git married? I'm worried about you. Settin' at breakfast, I looked at you real hard, and I seen you've got some grey hairs already."

"Oh, yes! They're coming. Maybe they'd come faster if I married."

"Don't talk so. You'll ruin your health eating at the hotel. I could send your wife a nice loaf of nut bread, if you only had one. I don't like to see a young man getting grey. I'll tell you something, Ed; you make some strong tea and keep it handy in a bowl, and every morning just brush it into your hair, an' it'll keep the grey from showin' much. That's the way I do!"

Sometimes the Doctor heard the gossipers in the drug-store wondering why Rosicky didn't get on faster. He was industrious, and so were his boys, but they were rather free and easy, weren't pushers, and they didn't always show good judgment. They were comfortable, they were out of debt, but they didn't get much ahead. Maybe, Doctor Burleigh reflected, people as generous and warm-hearted and affectionate as the Rosickys never got ahead much; maybe you couldn't enjoy your life and put it into the bank, too.

II

When Rosicky left Doctor Burleigh's office he went into the farm-implement store to light his pipe and put on his glasses and read over the list Mary had given him. Then he went into the general merchandise place next door and stood about until the pretty girl with the plucked eyebrows, who always waited on him, was free. Those eyebrows, two thin India-ink strokes, amused him, because he remembered how they used to be. Rosicky always prolonged his shopping by a little joking; the girl knew the old fellow admired her, and she liked to chaff with him.

"Seems to me about every other week you buy ticking, Mr. Rosicky, and always the best quality," she remarked as she measured off the heavy bolt with red stripes.

"You see, my wife is always makin' goose-fedder pillows, an' de thin stuff don't hold in dem little down-fedders."

"You must have lots of pillows at your house."

"Sure. She makes quilts of dem, too. We sleeps easy. Now she's makin' a fedder quilt for my son's wife. You know Polly, that married my Rudolph. How much my bill, Miss Pearl?"

"Eight eighty-five."

"Chust make it nine, and put in some candy fur de women."

"As usual. I never did see a man buy so much candy for his wife. First thing you know, she'll be getting too fat."

"I'd like dat. I ain't much fur all dem slim women like what de style is now."

"That's one for me, I suppose, Mr. Bohunk!" Pearl sniffed and elevated her India-ink strokes.

When Rosicky went out to his wagon, it was beginning to snow, — the first snow of the season, and he was glad to see it. He rattled out of town and along the highway through a wonderfully rich stretch of country, the finest farms in the county. He admired this High Prairie, as it was called, and always liked to drive through it. His own place lay in a rougher territory, where there was some clay in the soil and it was not so productive. When he bought his land, he hadn't the money to buy on High Prairie; so he told his boys, when they grumbled, that if their land hadn't some clay in it, they wouldn't own it at all. All the same, he enjoyed looking at these fine farms, as he enjoyed looking at a prize bull.

After he had gone eight miles, he came to the graveyard, which lay just at the edge of his own hay-land. There he stopped his horses and sat still on his wagon seat, looking about at the snowfall. Over yonder on the hill he could see his own house, crouching low, with the clump of orchard behind and the windmill before, and all down the gentle hill-slope the rows of pale gold cornstalks stood out against the white field. The snow was falling over the cornfield and the pasture and the hay-land, steadily, with very little wind, — a nice dry snow. The graveyard had only a light wire fence about it and was all overgrown with long red grass. The fine snow, settling into this red grass and upon the few little evergreens and the headstones, looked very pretty.

It was a nice graveyard, Rosicky reflected, sort of snug and homelike, not cramped or mournful, — a big sweep all round it. A man could lie down in the long grass and see the complete arch of the sky over him, hear the wagons go by; in summer the mowing-machine rattled right up to the wire fence. And it was so near home. Over there across the cornstalks his own roof and windmill looked so good to him that he promised himself to mind the Doctor and take care of himself. He was awful fond of his place, he admitted. He wasn't anxious to leave it. And it was a comfort to think that he would never have to go farther than the edge of his own hayfield. The snow, falling over his barnyard and the graveyard, seemed to draw things together like. And they were all old neighbours in the graveyard, most of them friends; there was nothing to feel awkward or embarrassed about. Embarrassment was the most disagreeable feeling Rosicky knew. He didn't often have it, — only with certain people whom he didn't understand at all.

Well, it was a nice snowstorm; a fine sight to see the snow falling so quietly and graciously over so much open country. On his cap and shoulders, on the horses' backs and manes, light, delicate, mysterious it fell; and with it a dry cool fragrance was released into the air. It meant rest for vegetation and men and beasts, for the ground itself; a season of long nights for sleep, leisurely breakfasts, peace by the fire. This and much more went through Rosicky's mind, but he merely told himself that winter was coming, clucked to his horses, and drove on.

When he reached home, John, the youngest boy, ran out to put away his team for him, and he met Mary coming up from the outside cellar with her apron full of carrots. They went into the house together. On the table, covered with oilcloth figured with clusters of blue grapes, a place was set, and he smelled hot coffee-cafe of some kind. Anton never lunched in town; he thought that extravagant, and anyhow he didn't like the food. So Mary always had something ready for him when he got home.

After he was settled in his chair, stirring his coffee in a big cup, Mary took out of the oven a pan of *kolache* stuffed with apricots, examined them anxiously to see whether they had got too dry, put them beside his plate, and then sat down opposite him.

Rosicky asked her in Czech if she wasn't going to have any coffee.

She replied in English, as being somehow the right language for transacting business: "Now what did Doctor Ed say, Anton? You tell me just what."

"He said I was to tell you some compliments, but I forgot 'em." Rosicky's eyes twinkled.

"About you, I mean. What did he say about your asthma?"

"He says I ain't got no asthma." Rosicky took one of the little rolls in his broad brown fingers. The thickened nail of his right thumb told the story of his past.

"Well, what is the matter? And don't try to put me off."

"He don't say nothing much, only I'm a little older, and my heart ain't so good like it used to be."

Mary started and brushed her hair back from her temples with both hands as if she were a little out of her mind. From the way she glared, she might have been in a rage with him.

"He says there's something the matter with your heart? Doctor Ed says so?"

"Now don't yell at me like I was a hog in de garden, Mary. You know I always did like to hear a woman talk soft. He didn't say anything de matter wid my heart, only it ain't so young like it used to be, an' he tell me not to pitch hay or run de corn-sheller."

Mary wanted to jump up, but she sat still. She admired the way he never under any circumstances raised his voice or spoke roughly. He was city-bred, and she was country-bred;

she often said she wanted her boys to have their papa's nice
ways.

"You never have no pain there, do you? It's your breathing
and your stomach that's been wrong. I wouldn't believe
nobody but Doctor Ed about it. I guess I'll go see him myself.
Didn't he give you no advice?"

"Chust to take it easy like, an' stay round de house dis
winter. I guess you got some carpenter work for me to do. I
kin make some new shelves for you, and I want dis long time
to build a closet in de boys' room and make dem two little
fellers keep dere clo'es hung up."

Rosicky drank his coffee from time to time, while he
considered. His moustache was of the soft long variety and
came down over his mouth like the teeth of a buggy-
rake over a bundle of hay. Each time he put down his cup,
he ran a blue handkerchief over his lips. When he took a
drink of water, he managed very neatly with the back of his
hand.

Mary sat watching him intently, trying to find any change
in his face. It is hard to see anyone who has become like your
own body to you. Yes, his hair had got thin, and his high
forehead had deep lines running from left to right. But his
neck, always clean shaved except in the busiest seasons, was
not loose or baggy. It was burned a dark reddish brown, and
there were deep creases in it, but it looked firm and full of
blood. His cheeks had a good colour. On either side of his
mouth there was a half-moon down the length of his cheek,
not wrinkles, but two lines that had come there from his
habitual expression. He was shorter and broader than when
she married him; his back had grown broad and curved, a
good deal like the shell of an old turtle, and his arms and
legs were short.

He was fifteen years older than Mary, but she had hardly
ever thought about it before. He was her man, and the kind
of man she liked. She was rough, and he was gentle, — city-

bred, as she always said. They had been shipmates on a rough voyage and had stood by each other in trying times. Life had gone well with them because, at bottom, they had the same ideas about life. They agreed, without discussion, as to what was most important and what was secondary. They didn't often exchange opinions, even in Czech, — it was as if they had thought the same thought together. A good deal had to be sacrificed and thrown overboard in a hard life like theirs, and they had never disagreed as to the things that could go. It had been a hard life, and a soft life, too. There wasn't anything brutal in the short, broad-backed man with the three-cornered eyes and the forehead that went on to the top of his skull. He was a city man, a gentle man, and though he had married a rough farm girl, he had never touched her without gentleness.

They had been at one accord not to hurry through life, not to be always skimping and saving. They saw their neighbours buy more land and feed more stock than they did, without discontent. Once when the creamery agent came to the Rosickys to persuade them to sell him their cream, he told them how much money the Fasslers, their nearest neighbours, had made on their cream last year.

"Yes," said Mary, "and look at them Fassler children! Pale, pinched little things, they look like skimmed milk. I'd rather put some colour into my children's faces than put money into the bank."

The agent shrugged and turned to Anton.

"I guess we'll do like she says," said Rosicky.

III

Mary very soon got into town to see Doctor Ed, and then she had a talk with her boys and set a guard over Rosicky. Even John, the youngest, had his father on his mind. If Rosicky went to throw hay down from the loft, one of the boys ran up the ladder and took the fork from him. He sometimes complained that though he was getting to be an old man, he wasn't an old woman yet.

That winter he stayed in the house in the afternoons and carpentered, or sat in the chair between the window full of plants and the wooden bench where the two pails of drinking water stood. This spot was called "Father's corner," though it was not a corner at all. He had a shelf there, where he kept his Bohemian papers and his pipes and tobacco, and his shears and needles and thread and tailor's thimble. Having been a tailor in his youth, he couldn't bear to see a woman patching at his clothes, or at the boys'. He liked tailoring, and always patched all the overalls and jackets and work shirts. Occasionally he made over a pair of pants one of the older boys had outgrown, for the little fellow.

While he sewed, he let his mind run back over his life. He had a good deal to remember, really; life in three countries. The only part of his youth he didn't like to remember was the two years he had spent in London, in Cheapside, working for a German tailor who was wretchedly poor. Those days, when he was nearly always hungry, when his clothes were dropping off him for dirt, and the sound of a strange language kept him in continual bewilderment, had left a sore spot in his mind that wouldn't bear touching.

He was twenty when he landed at Castle Garden in New York, and he had a protector who got him work in a tailor shop in Vesey Street, down near the Washington Market. He looked upon that part of his life as very happy. He became a good workman, he was industrious, and his wages were increased from time to time. He minded his own business and envied nobody's good fortune. He went to night school and learned to read English. He often did overtime work and was well paid for it, but somehow he never saved anything. He couldn't refuse a loan to a friend, and he was self-indulgent. He liked a good dinner, and a little went for beer, a little for tobacco; a good deal went to the girls. He often stood through an opera on Saturday nights; he could get standing-room for a dollar. Those were the great days of opera in New York, and it gave a fellow something to think about for the rest of the week. Rosicky had a quick ear, and a childish love of all the stage splendour; the scenery, the costumes, the ballet. He usually went with a chum, and after the performance they had beer and maybe some oysters somewhere. It was a fine life; for the first five years or so it satisfied him completely. He was never hungry or cold or dirty, and everything amused him: a fire, a dog fight, a parade, a storm, a ferry ride. He thought New York the finest, richest, friendliest city in the world.

Moreover, he had what he called a happy home life. Very near the tailor shop was a small furniture-factory, where an old Austrian, Loeffler, employed a few skilled men and made unusual furniture, most of it to order, for the rich German housewives up-town. The top floor of Loeffler's five-storey factory was a loft, where he kept his choice lumber and stored the odd pieces of furniture left on his hands. One of the young workmen he employed was a Czech, and he and Rosicky became fast friends. They persuaded Loeffler to let them have a sleeping-room in one corner of the loft. They bought good beds and bedding and had their pick of the furniture kept up there. The loft was low-pitched, but light and airy, full of windows, and good-smelling by reason of the fine lumber put up there to season. Old Loeffler used to go down to the docks and buy wood from South America and the East from the sea captains. The young men were as foolish about their house as a bridal pair. Zichec, the young cabinet-maker, devised every sort of convenience, and Rosicky kept their clothes in order. At night and on Sundays, when the quiver of machinery underneath was still, it was the quietest place in the world, and on summer nights all the sea winds blew in. Zichec often practised on his flute in the evening. They were both fond of music and went to the opera together. Rosicky thought he wanted to live like that forever.

But as the years passed, all alike, he began to get a little restless. When spring came round, he would begin to feel fretted, and he got to drinking. He was likely to drink too much of a Saturday night. On Sunday he was languid and heavy, getting over his spree. On Monday he plunged into work again. So he never had time to figure out what ailed him, though he knew something did. When the grass turned green in Park Place, and the lilac hedge at the back of Trinity churchyard put out its blossoms, he was tormented by a longing to run away. That was why he drank too much; to get a temporary illusion of freedom and wide horizons.

Rosicky, the old Rosicky, could remember as if it were yesterday the day when the young Rosicky found out what was the matter with him. It was on a Fourth of July afternoon, and he was sitting in Park Place in the sun. The lower part of New York was empty. Wall Street, Liberty Street, Broadway, all empty. So much stone and asphalt with nothing going on, so many empty windows. The emptiness was intense, like the stillness in a great factory when the machinery stops and the belts and bands cease running. It was too great a change, it took all the strength out of one. Those blank buildings, without the stream of life pouring through them, were like empty jails. It struck young Rosicky that this was the trouble with big cities; they built you in from the earth itself, cemented you away from any contact with the ground. You lived in an unnatural world, like the fish in an aquarium, who were probably much more comfortable than they ever were in the sea.

On that very day he began to think seriously about the articles he had read in the Bohemian papers, describing prosperous Czech farming communities in the West. He believed he would like to go out there as a farm hand; it was hardly possible that he could ever have land of his own. His people had always been workmen; his father and grandfather had worked in shops. His mother's parents had lived in the country, but they rented their farm and had a hard time to get along. Nobody in his family had ever owned any land, — that belonged to a different station of life altogether. Anton's mother died when he was little, and he was sent into the country to her parents. He stayed with them until he was twelve, and formed those ties with the earth and the farm animals and growing things which are never made at all unless they are made early. After his grandfather died, he went back to live with his father and stepmother, but she was very hard on him, and his father helped him to get passage to London.

After that Fourth of July day in Park Place, the desire to return to the country never left him. To work on another man's farm would be all he asked; to see the sun rise and set and to plant things and watch them grow. He was a very simple man. He was like a tree that has not many roots, but one tap-root that goes down deep. He subscribed for a Bohemian paper printed in Chicago, then for one printed in Omaha. His mind got farther and farther west. He began to save a little money to buy his liberty. When he was thirty-five, there was a great meeting in New York of Bohemian athletic societies, and Rosicky left the tailor shop and went home with the Omaha delegates to try his fortune in another part of the world.

IV

Perhaps the fact that his own youth was well over before he began to have a family was one reason why Rosicky was so fond of his boys. He had almost a grandfather's indulgence for them. He had never had to worry about any of them — except, just now, a little about Rudolph.

On Saturday night the boys always piled into the Ford, took little Josephine, and went to town to the moving-picture show. One Saturday morning they were talking at the breakfast table about starting early that evening, so that they would have an hour or so to see the Christmas things in the stores before the show began. Rosicky looked down the table.

"I hope you boys ain't disappointed, but I want you to let me have de car tonight. Maybe some of you can go in with de neighbours."

Their faces fell. They worked hard all week, and they were still like children. A new jackknife or a box of candy pleased the older ones as much as the little fellow.

"If you and Mother are going to town," Frank said, "maybe you could take a couple of us along with you, anyway."

"No, I want to take de car down to Rudolph's, and let him an' Polly go in to de show. She don't git into town enough, an' I'm afraid she's gettin' lonesome, an' he can't afford no car yet."

That settled it. The boys were a good deal dashed. Their father took another piece of apple-cake and went on: "Maybe next Saturday night de two little fellers can go along wid dem."

"Oh, is Rudolph going to have the car every Saturday night?"

Rosicky did not reply at once; then he began to speak seriously: "Listen, boys; Polly ain't lookin' so good. I don't like to see nobody lookin' sad. It comes hard fur a town girl to be a farmer's wife. I don't want no trouble to start in Rudolph's family. When it starts, it ain't so easy to stop. An American girl don't git used to our ways all at once. I like to tell Polly she and Rudolph can have the car every Saturday night till after New Year's, if it's all right with you boys."

"Sure it's all right, Papa," Mary cut in. "And it's good you thought about that. Town girls is used to more than country girls. I lay awake nights, scared she'll make Rudolph discontented with the farm."

The boys put as good a face on it as they could. They surely looked forward to their Saturday nights in town. That evening Rosicky drove the car the half-mile down to Rudolph's new, bare little house.

Polly was in a short-sleeved gingham dress, clearing away the supper dishes. She was a trim, slim little thing, with blue eyes and shingled yellow hair, and her eyebrows were reduced to a mere brush-stroke, like Miss Pearl's.

"Good evening, Mr. Rosicky. Rudolph's at the barn, I guess." She never called him father, or Mary mother. She was sensitive about having married a foreigner. She never in the world would have done it if Rudolph hadn't been such a handsome, persuasive fellow and such a gallant lover. He had graduated in her class in the high school in town, and their friendship began in the ninth grade.

Rosicky went in, though he wasn't exactly asked. "My boys ain't goin' to town tonight, an' I brought de car over fur you two to go in to de picture show."

Polly, carrying dishes to the sink, looked over her shoulder at him. "Thank you. But I'm late with my work tonight, and pretty tired. Maybe Rudolph would like to go in with you."

"Oh, I don't go to de shows! I'm too old-fashioned. You won't feel so tired after you ride in de air a ways. It's a nice clear night, an' it ain't cold. You go an' fix yourself up, Polly, an' I'll wash de dishes an' leave everything nice fur you."

Polly blushed and tossed her bob. "I couldn't let you do that, Mr. Rosicky. I wouldn't think of it."

Rosicky said nothing. He found a bib apron on a nail behind the kitchen door. He slipped it over his head and then took Polly by her two elbows and pushed her gently toward the door of her own room. "I washed up de kitchen many times for my wife, when de babies was sick or somethin'. You go an' make yourself look nice. I like you to look prettier'n any of dem town girls when you go in. De young folks must have some fun, an' I'm goin' to look out fur you, Polly."

That kind, reassuring grip on her elbows, the old man's funny bright eyes, made Polly want to drop her head on his shoulder for a second. She restrained herself, but she lingered in his grasp at the door of her room, murmuring tearfully: "You always lived in the city when you were young, didn't you? Don't you ever get lonesome out here?"

As she turned round to him, her hand fell naturally into his, and he stood holding it and smiling into her face with his peculiar, knowing, indulgent smile without a shadow of reproach in it. "Dem big cities is all right fur de rich, but dey is terrible hard fur de poor."

"I don't know. Sometimes I think I'd like to take a chance. You lived in New York, didn't you?"

"An' London. Da's bigger still. I learned my trade dere. Here's Rudolph comin', you better hurry."

"Will you tell me about London some time?"

"Maybe. Only I ain't no talker, Polly. Run an' dress yourself up."

The bedroom door closed behind her, and Rudolph came in from the outside, looking anxious. He had seen the car and was sorry any of his family should come just then. Supper hadn't been a very pleasant occasion. Halting in the doorway, he saw his father in a kitchen apron, carrying dishes to the sink. He flushed crimson and something flashed in his eye. Rosicky held up a warning finger.

"I brought de car over fur you an' Polly to go to de picture show, an' I made her let me finish here so you won't be late. You go put on a clean shirt, quick!"

"But don't the boys want the car, Father?"

"Not tonight dey don't." Rosicky fumbled under his apron and found his pants pocket. He took out a silver dollar and said in a hurried whisper: "You go an' buy dat girl some ice cream an' candy tonight, like you was courtin'. She's awful good friends wid me."

Rudolph was very short of cash, but he took the money as if it hurt him. There had been a crop failure all over the county. He had more than once been sorry he'd married this year.

In a few minutes the young people came out, looking clean and a little stiff. Rosicky hurried them off, and then he took his own time with the dishes. He scoured the pots and pans and put away the milk and swept the kitchen. He put some coal in the stove and shut off the draughts, so the place would be warm for them when they got home late at night. Then he sat down and had a pipe and listened to the clock tick.

Generally speaking, marrying an American girl was certainly a risk. A Czech should marry a Czech. It was lucky that Polly was the daughter of a poor widow woman; Rudolph was proud, and if she had a prosperous family to throw up at him, they could never make it go. Polly was one of four sisters, and they all worked; one was book-keeper in the bank, one taught music, and Polly and her younger sister had been clerks, like Miss Pearl. All four of them were musical, had pretty voices, and sang in the Methodist choir, which the eldest sister directed.

Polly missed the sociability of a store position. She missed the choir, and the company of her sisters. She didn't dislike housework, but she disliked so much of it. Rosicky was a little anxious about this pair. He was afraid Polly would grow so discontented that Rudy would quit the farm and take a factory job in Omaha. He had worked for a winter up there, two years ago, to get money to marry on. He had done very well, and they would always take him back at the stockyards. But to Rosicky that meant the end of everything for his son. To be a landless man was to be a wage-earner, a slave, all your life; to have nothing, to be nothing.

Rosicky thought he would come over and do a little carpentering for Polly after the New Year. He guessed she needed jollying. Rudolph was a serious sort of chap, serious in love and serious about his work.

Rosicky shook out his pipe and walked home across the fields. Ahead of him the lamplight shone from his kitchen windows. Suppose he were still in a tailor shop on Vesey Street, with a bunch of pale, narrow-chested sons working on machines, all coming home tired and sullen to eat supper in a kitchen that was a parlour also; with another crowded, angry family quarrelling just across the dumb-waiter shaft, and squeaking pulleys at the windows where dirty washings hung on dirty lines above a court full of old brooms and mops and ash-cans. . . .

He stopped by the windmill to look up at the frosty winter stars and draw a long breath before he went inside. That kitchen with the shining windows was dear to him; but the sleeping fields and bright stars and the noble darkness were dearer still.

V

On the day before Christmas the weather set in very cold; no snow, but a bitter, biting wind that whistled and sang over the flat land and lashed one's face like fine wires. There was baking going on in the Rosicky kitchen all day, and Rosicky sat inside, making over a coat that Albert had outgrown into an overcoat for John. Mary had a big red geranium in bloom for Christmas, and a row of Jerusalem cherry trees, full of berries. It was the first year she had ever grown these; Doctor Ed brought her the seeds from Omaha when he went to some medical convention. They reminded Rosicky of plants he had seen in England; and all afternoon, as he stitched, he sat thinking about those two years in London, which his mind usually shrank from even after all this while.

He was a lad of eighteen when he dropped down into
London, with no money and no connexions except the
address of a cousin who was supposed to be working at a
confectioner's. When he went to the pastry shop, however,
he found that the cousin had gone to America. Anton
tramped the streets for several days, sleeping in doorways
and on the Embankment, until he was in utter despair. He
knew no English, and the sound of the strange language all
about him confused him. By chance he met a poor German
tailor who had learned his trade in Vienna, and could speak
a little Czech. This tailor, Lifschnitz, kept a repair shop in a
Cheapside basement, underneath a cobbler. He didn't much
need an apprentice, but he was sorry for the boy and took
him in for no wages but his keep and what he could pick up.
The pickings were supposed to be coppers given you when
you took work home to a customer. But most of the
customers called for their clothes themselves, and the coppers
that came Anton's way were very few. He had, however, a
place to sleep. The tailor's family lived upstairs in three
rooms; a kitchen, a bedroom, where Lifschnitz and his wife
and five children slept, and a living-room. Two corners of
this living-room were curtained off for lodgers; in one
Rosicky slept on an old horsehair sofa, with a feather quilt
to wrap himself in. The other corner was rented to a
wretched, dirty boy, who was studying the violin. He actually
practised there. Rosicky was dirty, too. There was no way to
be anything else. Mrs. Lifschnitz got the water she cooked
and washed with from a pump in a brick court, four flights
down. There were bugs in the place, and multitudes of fleas,
though the poor woman did the best she could. Rosicky knew
she often went empty to give another potato or a spoonful
of dripping to the two hungry, sad-eyed boys who lodged
with her. He used to think he would never get out of there,
never get a clean shirt to his back again. What would he do,
he wondered, when his clothes actually dropped to pieces

and the worn cloth wouldn't hold patches any longer?

It was still early when the old farmer put aside his sewing and his recollections. The sky had been a dark grey all day, with not a gleam of sun, and the light failed at four o'clock. He went to shave and change his shirt while the turkey was roasting. Rudolph and Polly were coming over for supper.

After supper they sat round in the kitchen, and the younger boys were saying how sorry they were it hadn't snowed. Everybody was sorry. They wanted a deep snow that would lie long and keep the wheat warm, and leave the ground soaked when it melted.

"Yes, sir!" Rudolph broke out fiercely; "if we have another dry year like last year, there's going to be hard times in this country."

Rosicky filled his pipe. "You boys don't know what hard times is. You don't owe nobody, you got plenty to eat an' keep warm, an' plenty water to keep clean. When you got them, you can't have it very hard."

Rudolph frowned, opened and shut his big right hand, and dropped it clenched upon his knee. "I've got to have a good deal more than that, Father, or I'll quit this farming gamble. I can always make good wages railroading, or at the packing house, and be sure of my money."

"Maybe so," his father answered dryly.

Mary, who had just come in from the pantry and was wiping her hands on the roller towel, thought Rudy and his father were getting too serious. She brought her darning-basket and sat down in the middle of the group.

"I ain't much afraid of hard times, Rudy," she said heartily. "We've had a plenty, but we've always come through. Your father wouldn't never take nothing very hard, not even hard times. I got a mind to tell you a story on him. Maybe you boys can't hardly remember the year we had that terrible hot wind, that burned everything up on the Fourth of July? All the corn an' the gardens. An' that was in the days when we didn't have alfalfa yet, — I guess it wasn't invented.

"Well, that very day your father was out cultivatin' corn, and I was here in the kitchen makin' plum preserves. We had bushels of plums that year. I noticed it was terrible hot, but it's always hot in the kitchen when you're preservin', an' I was too busy with my plums to mind. Anton come in from the field about three o'clock, an' I asked him what was the matter.

"'Nothin',' he says, 'but it's pretty hot, an' I think I won't work no more today.' He stood round for a few minutes, an' then he says: 'Ain't you near through? I want you should git up a nice supper for us tonight. It's Fourth of July.'

"I told him to git along, that I was right in the middle of preservin', but the plums would taste good on hot biscuit. 'I'm goin' to have fried chicken, too,' he says, and he went off an' killed a couple. You three oldest boys was little fellers, playin' round outside, real hot an' sweaty, an' your father took you to the horse tank down by the windmill an' took off your clothes an' put you in. Them two box-elder trees was little then, but they made shade over the tank. Then he took off all his own clothes, an' got in with you. While he was playin' in the water with you, the Methodist preacher drove into our place to say how all the neighbours was goin' to meet at the schoolhouse that night, to pray for rain. He drove right to the windmill, of course, and there was your father and you three with no clothes on. I was in the kitchen door, an' I had to laugh, for the preacher acted like he ain't never seen a naked man before. He surely was embarrassed, an' your father couldn't git to his clothes; they was all hangin' up on the windmill to let the sweat dry out of 'em. So he laid in the tank where he was, an' put one of you boys on top of him to cover him up a little, an' talked to the preacher.

"When you got through playin' in the water, he put clean clothes on you and a clean shirt on himself, an' by that time

I'd begun to get supper. He says: 'It's too hot in here to eat comfortable. Let's have a picnic in the orchard. We'll eat our supper behind the mulberry hedge, under them linden trees.'

"So he carried our supper down, an' a bottle of my wild-grape wine, an' everything tasted good, I can tell you. The wind got cooler as the sun was goin' down, and it turned out pleasant, only I noticed how the leaves was curled up on the linden trees. That made me think, an' I asked your father if that hot wind all day hadn't been terrible hard on the gardens an' the corn.

"'Corn,' he says, 'there ain't no corn.'

"'What you talkin' about?' I said. 'Ain't we got forty acres?'

"'We ain't got an ear,' he says, 'nor nobody else ain't got none. All the corn in this country was cooked by three o'clock today, like you'd roasted it in an oven.'

"'You mean you won't get no crop at all?' I asked him. I couldn't believe it, after he'd worked so hard.

"'No crop this year,' he says. 'That's why we're havin' a picnic. We might as well enjoy what we got.'

"An' that's how your father behaved, when all the neighbours was so discouraged they couldn't look you in the face. An' we enjoyed ourselves that year, poor as we was, an' our neighbours wasn't a bit better off for bein' miserable. Some of 'em grieved till they got poor digestions and couldn't relish what they did have."

The younger boys said they thought their father had the best of it. But Rudolph was thinking that, all the same, the neighbours had managed to get ahead more, in the fifteen years since that time. There must be something wrong about his father's way of doing things. He wished he knew what was going on in the back of Polly's mind. He knew she liked his father, but he knew, too, that she was afraid of something. When his mother sent over coffee-cake or prune tarts or a loaf of fresh bread, Polly seemed to regard them with a certain suspicion. When she observed to him that his brothers had nice manners, her tone implied that it was remarkable they should have. With his mother she was stiff and on her guard. Mary's hearty frankness and gusts of good humour irritated her. Polly was afraid of being unusual or conspicuous in any way, of being "ordinary," as she said!

When Mary had finished her story, Rosicky laid aside his pipe.

"You boys like me to tell you about some of dem hard times I been through in London?" Warmly encouraged, he sat rubbing his forehead along the deep creases. It was bothersome to tell a long story in English (he nearly always talked to the boys in Czech), but he wanted Polly to hear this one.

"Well, you know about dat tailor shop I worked in in London? I had one Christmas dere I ain't never forgot. Times was awful bad before Christmas; de boss ain't got much work, an' have it awful hard to pay his rent. It ain't so much fun, bein' poor in a big city like London, I'll say! All de windows is full of good t'ings to eat, an' all de pushcarts in de streets is full, an' you smell 'em all de time, an' you ain't got no money, — not a damn bit. I didn't mind de cold so much, though I didn't have no overcoat, chust a short jacket I'd outgrowed so it wouldn't meet on me, an' my hands was chapped raw. But I always had a good appetite, like you all know, an' de sight of dem pork pies in de windows was awful fur me!

"Day before Christmas was terrible foggy dat year, an' dat fog gits into your bones and makes you all damp like. Mrs. Lifschnitz didn't give us nothin' but a little bread an' drippin' for supper, because she was savin' to try for to give us a good dinner on Christmas Day. After supper de boss say I can go an' enjoy myself, so I went into de streets to listen to de Christmas singers. Dey sing old songs an' make very nice music, an' I run round after dem a good ways, till I got awful hungry. I t'ink maybe if I go home, I can sleep till morning an' forgit my belly.

"I went into my corner real quiet, and roll up in my fedder quilt. But I ain't got my head down, till I smell somet'ing good. Seem like it git stronger an' stronger, an' I can't git to sleep noway. I can't understand dat smell. Dere was a gas light in a hall across de court, dat always shine in at my window a little. I got up an' look round. I got a little wooden box in my corner fur a stool, 'cause I ain't got no chair. I picks up dat box, and under it dere is a roast goose on a platter! I can't believe my eyes. I carry it to de window where de light comes in, an' touch it and smell it to find out, an' den I taste it to be sure. I say, I will eat chust one little bite of dat goose, so I can go to sleep, and tomorrow I won't eat none at all. But I tell you, boys, when I stop, one half of dat goose was gone!"

The narrator bowed his head, and the boys shouted. But little Josephine slipped behind his chair and kissed him on the neck beneath his ear.

"Poor little Papa, I don't want him to be hungry!"

"Da's long ago, child. I ain't never been hungry since I had your mudder to cook fur me."

"Go on and tell us the rest, please," said Polly.

"Well, when I come to realize what I done, of course, I felt terrible. I felt better in de stomach, but very bad in de heart. I set on my bed wid dat platter on my knees, an' it all come to me; how hard dat poor woman save to buy dat goose, and how she get some neighbour to cook it dat got more fire, an' how she put it in my corner to keep it away from dem hungry children. Dey was a old carpet hung up to shut my corner off, an' de children wasn't allowed to go in dere. An' I know she put it in my corner because she trust me more'n she did de violin boy. I can't stand it to face her after I spoil de Christmas. So I put on my shoes and go out into de city. I tell myself I better throw myself in de river; but I guess I ain't dat kind of a boy.

"It was after twelve o'clock, an' terrible cold, an' I start out to walk about London all night. I walk along de river awhile, but dey was lots of drunks all along; men, and women too. I chust move along to keep away from de police. I git onto de Strand, an' den over to New Oxford Street, where dere was a big German restaurant on de ground floor, wid big windows all fixed up fine, an' I could see de people havin' parties inside. While I was lookin' in, two men and two ladies come out, laughin' and talkin' and feelin' happy about all dey been eatin' an' drinkin', and dey was speakin' Czech, — not like de Austrians, but like de home folks talk it.

"I guess I went crazy, an' I done what I ain't never done before nor since. I went right up to dem gay people an' begun to beg dem: 'Fellow-countrymen, for God's sake give me money enough to buy a goose!'

"Dey laugh, of course, but de ladies speak awful kind to me, an' dey take me back into de restaurant and give me hot coffee and cakes, an' make me tell all about how I happened to come to London, an' what I was doin' dere. Dey take my name and where I work down on paper, an' both of dem ladies give me ten shillings.

"De big market at Covent Garden ain't very far away, an' by dat time it was open. I go dere an' buy a big goose an' some pork pies, an' potatoes and onions, an' cakes an' oranges fur de children, — all I could carry! When I git home, everybody is still asleep. I pile all I bought on de kitchen table, an' go in an' lay down on my bed, an' I ain't waken up till I hear dat woman scream when she come out into her kitchen. My goodness, but she was surprise! She laugh an' cry at de same time, an' hug me and waken all de children. She ain't stop fur no breakfast; she git de Christmas dinner ready dat morning, and we all sit down an' eat all we can hold. I ain't never seen dat violin boy have all he can hold before.

"Two three days after dat, de two men come to hunt me up, an' dey ask my boss, and he give me a good report an' tell dem I was a steady boy all right. One of dem Bohemians was very smart an' run a Bohemian newspaper in New York, an' de odder was a rich man, in dc importing business, an' dey been travelling togedder. Dey told me how t'ings was easier in New York, an' offered to pay my passage when dey was goin' home soon on a boat. My boss say to me: 'You go. You ain't got no chance here, an' I like to see you git ahead, fur you always been a good boy to my woman, and fur dat fine Christmas dinner you give us all.' An' da's how I got to New York."

That night when Rudolph and Polly, arm in arm, were running home across the fields with the bitter wind at their backs, his heart leaped for joy when she said she thought they might have his family come over for supper on New Year's Eve. "Let's get up a nice supper, and not let your mother help at all; make her be company for once."

"That would be lovely of you, Polly," he said humbly. He was a very simple, modest boy, and he, too, felt vaguely that Polly and her sisters were more experienced and worldly than his people.

VI

The winter turned out badly for farmers. It was bitterly cold, and after the first light snows before Christmas there was no snow at all, — and no rain. March was as bitter as February. On those days when the wind fairly punished the country, Rosicky sat by his window. In the fall he and the boys had put in a big wheat planting, and now the seed had frozen in the ground. All that land would have to be ploughed up and planted over again, planted in corn. It had happened before, but he was younger then, and he never worried about what had to be. He was sure of himself and of Mary; he knew they could bear what they had to bear, that they would always pull through somehow. But he was not so sure about the young ones, and he felt troubled because Rudolph and Polly were having such a hard start.

Sitting beside his flowering window while the panes rattled and the wind blew in under the door, Rosicky gave himself to reflection as he had not done since those Sundays in the loft of the furniture-factory in New York, long ago. Then he was trying to find what he wanted in life for himself; now he was trying to find what he wanted for his boys, and why it was he so hungered to feel sure they would be here, working this very land, after he was gone.

They would have to work hard on the farm, and probably they would never do much more than make a living. But if he could think of them as staying here on the land, he wouldn't have to fear any great unkindness for them. Hardships, certainly; it was a hardship to have the wheat freeze in the ground when seed was so high; and to have to sell your stock because you had no feed. But there would be other years when everything came along right, and you caught up. And what you had was your own. You didn't have to choose between bosses and strikers, and go wrong either way. You didn't have to do with dishonest and cruel people. They were the only things in his experience he had found terrifying and horrible; the look in the eyes of a dishonest and crafty man, of a scheming and rapacious woman.

In the country, if you had a mean neighbour, you could keep off his land and make him keep off yours. But in the city, all the foulness and misery and brutality of your neighbours was part of your life. The worst things he had come upon in his journey through the world were human, — depraved and poisonous specimens of man. To this day he could recall certain terrible faces in the London streets. There

were mean people everywhere, to be sure, even in their own
country town here. But they weren't tempered, hardened,
sharpened, like the treacherous people in cities who live by
grinding or cheating or poisoning their fellow-men. He had
helped to bury two of his fellow-workmen in the tailoring
trade, and he was distrustful of the organized industries that
see one out of the world in big cities. Here, if you were sick,
you had Doctor Ed to look after you; and if you died, fat
Mr. Haycock, the kindest man in the world, buried you.

It seemed to Rosicky that for good, honest boys like his,
the worst they could do on the farm was better than the best
they would be likely to do in the city. If he'd had a mean
boy, now, who was crooked and sharp and tried to put
anything over on his brothers, then town would be the place
for him. But he had no such boy. As for Rudolph, the
discontented one, he would give the shirt off his back to
anyone who touched his heart. What Rosicky really hoped
for his boys was that they could get through the world
without ever knowing much about the cruelty of human
beings. "Their mother and me ain't prepared them for that,"
he sometimes said to himself.

These thoughts brought him back to a grateful consideration of his own case. What an escape he had had, to be sure!
He, too, in his time, had had to take money for repair work
from the hand of a hungry child who let it go so wistfully;
because it was money due his boss. And now, in all these
years, he had never had to take a cent from any one in bitter
need, — never had to look at the face of a woman become
like a wolf's from struggle and famine. When he thought of
these things, Rosicky would put on his cap and jacket and
slip down to the barn and give his work-horses a little extra
oats, letting them eat it out of his hand in their slobbery
fashion. It was his way of expressing what he felt, and made
him chuckle with pleasure.

The spring came warm, with blue skies, — but dry, dry as

a bone. The boys began ploughing up the wheat-fields to plant them over in corn. Rosicky would stand at the fence corner and watch them, and the earth was so dry it blew up in clouds of brown dust that hid the horses and the sulky plough and the driver. It was a bad outlook.

The big alfalfa-field that lay between the home place and Rudolph's came up green, but Rosicky was worried because during that open windy winter a great many Russian thistle plants had blown in there and lodged. He kept asking the boys to rake them out; he was afraid their seed would root and "take the alfalfa." Rudolph said that was nonsense. The boys were working so hard planting corn, their father felt he couldn't insist about the thistles, but he set great store by that big alfalfa field. It was a feed you could depend on, — and there was some deeper reason, vague, but strong. The peculiar green of that clover woke early memories in old Rosicky, went back to something in his childhood in the old world. When he was a little boy, he had played in fields of that strong blue-green colour.

One morning, when Rudolph had gone to town in the car, leaving a work-team idle in his barn, Rosicky went over to his son's place, put the horses to the buggy-rake, and set about quietly raking up those thistles. He behaved with guilty caution, and rather enjoyed stealing a march on Doctor Ed, who was just then taking his first vacation in seven years of practice and was attending a clinic in Chicago. Rosicky got the thistles raked up, but did not stop to burn them. That would take some time, and his breath was pretty short, so he thought he had better get the horses back to the barn.

He got them into the barn and to their stalls, but the pain had come on so sharp in his chest that he didn't try to take the harness off. He started for the house, bending lower with every step. The cramp in his chest was shutting him up like a jack-knife. When he reached the windmill, he swayed and caught at the ladder. He saw Polly coming down the hill, running with the swiftness of a slim greyhound. In a flash she had her shoulder under his armpit.

"Lean on me, Father, hard! Don't be afraid. We can get to the house all right!"

Somehow they did, though Rosicky became blind with pain; he could keep on his legs, but he couldn't steer his course. The next thing he was conscious of was lying on Polly's bed, and Polly bending over him wringing out bath towels in hot water and putting them on his chest. She stopped only to throw coal into the stove, and she kept the tea-kettle and the black pot going. She put these hot applications on him for nearly an hour, she told him afterwards, and all that time he was drawn up stiff and blue, with the sweat pouring off him.

As the pain gradually loosed its grip, the stiffness went out of his jaws, the black circles round his eyes disappeared, and a little of his natural colour came back. When his daughter-in-law buttoned his shirt over his chest at last, he sighed.

"Da's fine, de way I feel now, Polly. It was a awful bad spell, an' I was so sorry it all come on you like it did."

Polly was flushed and excited. "Is the pain really gone? Can I leave you long enough to telephone over to your place?"

Rosicky's eyelids fluttered. "Don't telephone, Polly. It ain't no use to scare my wife. It's nice and quiet here, an' if I ain't too much trouble to you, just let me lay still till I feel like myself. I ain't got no pain now. It's nice here."

Polly bent over him and wiped the moisture from his face. "Oh, I'm so glad it's over!" she broke out impulsively. "It just broke my heart to see you suffer so, Father."

Rosicky motioned her to sit down on the chair where the tea-kettle had been, and looked up at her with that lively affectionate gleam in his eyes. "You was awful good to me, I won't never forgit dat. I hate it to be sick on you like dis. Down at de barn I say to myself, dat young girl ain't had

much experience in sickness, I don't want to scare her, an'
maybe she's got a baby comin' or somet'ing."

Polly took his hand. He was looking at her so intently and
affectionately and confidingly; his eyes seemed to caress her
face, to regard it with pleasure. She frowned with her funny
streaks of eyebrows, and then smiled back at him.

"I guess maybe there is something of that kind going to
happen. But I haven't told anyone yet, not my mother or
Rudolph. You'll be the first to know."

His hand pressed hers. She noticed that it was warm again.
The twinkle in his yellow-brown eyes seemed to come nearer.

"I like mighty well to see dat little child, Polly," was all he
said. Then he closed his eyes and lay half-smiling. But Polly
sat still, thinking hard. She had a sudden feeling that nobody
in the world, not her mother, not Rudolph, or anyone, really
loved her as much as old Rosicky did. It perplexed her. She
sat frowning and trying to puzzle it out. It was as if Rosicky
had a special gift for loving people, something that was like
an ear for music or an eye for colour. It was quiet, unobtru-
sive; it was merely there. You saw it in his eyes, — perhaps
that was why they were merry. You felt it in his hands, too.
After he dropped off to sleep, she sat holding his warm,
broad, flexible brown hand. She had never seen another in
the least like it. She wondered if it wasn't a kind of gypsy
hand, it was so alive and quick and light in its communica-
tions, — very strange in a farmer. Nearly all the farmers she
knew had huge lumps of fists, like mauls, or they were knotty
and bony and uncomfortable-looking, with stiff fingers. But
Rosicky's was like quicksilver, flexible, muscular, about the
colour of a pale cigar, with deep, deep creases across the
palm. It wasn't nervous, it wasn't a stupid lump; it was a
warm brown human hand, with some cleverness in it, a great
deal of generosity, and something else which Polly could only
call "gypsy-like," — something nimble and lively and sure,
in the way that animals are.

Polly remembered that hour long afterwards; it had been like an awakening to her. It seemed to her that she had never learned so much about life from anything as from old Rosicky's hand. It brought her to herself; it communicated some direct and untranslatable message.

When she heard Rudolph coming in the car, she ran out to meet him.

"Oh, Rudy, your father's been awful sick! He raked up those thistles he's been worrying about, and afterwards he could hardly get to the house. He suffered so I was afraid he was going to die."

Rudolph jumped to the ground. "Where is he now?"

"On the bed. He's asleep. I was terribly scared, because, you know, I'm so fond of your father." She slipped her arm through his and they went into the house. That afternoon they took Rosicky home and put him to bed, though he protested that he was quite well again.

The next morning he got up and dressed and sat down to breakfast with his family. He told Mary that his coffee tasted better than usual to him, and he warned the boys not to bear any tales to Doctor Ed when he got home. After breakfast he sat down by his window to do some patching and asked Mary to thread several needles for him before she went to feed her chickens, — her eyes were better than his, and her hands steadier. He lit his pipe and took up John's overalls. Mary had been watching him anxiously all morning, and as she went out of the door with her bucket of scraps, she saw that he was smiling. He was thinking, indeed, about Polly, and how he might never have known what a tender heart she had if he hadn't got sick over there. Girls nowadays didn't wear their heart on their sleeve. But now he knew Polly would make a fine woman after the foolishness wore off. Either a woman had that sweetness at her heart or she hadn't. You couldn't always tell by the look of them; but if they had that, everything came out right in the end.

After he had taken a few stitches, the cramp began in his chest, like yesterday. He put his pipe cautiously down on the window-sill and bent over to ease the pull. No use, — he had better try to get to his bed if he could. He rose and groped his way across the familiar floor, which was rising and falling like the deck of a ship. At the door he fell. When Mary came in, she found him lying there, and the moment she touched him she knew that he was gone.

Doctor Ed was away when Rosicky died, and for the first few weeks after he got home he was hard driven. Every day he said to himself that he must get out to see that family that had lost their father. One soft, warm moonlight night in early summer he started for the farm. His mind was on other things, and not until his road ran by the graveyard did he realize that Rosicky wasn't over there on the hill where the red lamplight shone, but here, in the moonlight. He stopped his car, shut off the engine, and sat there for a while.

A sudden hush had fallen on his soul. Everything here seemed strangely moving and significant, though signifying what, he did not know. Close by the wire fence stood Rosicky's mowing-machine, where one of the boys had been cutting hay that afternoon; his own work-horses had been going up and down there. The new-cut hay perfumed all the night air. The moonlight silvered the long, billowy grass that grew over the graves and hid the fence; the few little evergreens stood out black in it, like shadows in a pool. The sky was very blue and soft, the stars rather faint because the moon was full.

For the first time it struck Doctor Ed that this was really a beautiful graveyard. He thought of city cemeteries; acres of shrubbery and heavy stone, so arranged and lonely and unlike anything in the living world. Cities of the dead, indeed; cities of the forgotten, of the "put away." But this was open and free, this little square of long grass which the wind for ever stirred. Nothing but the sky overhead, and the many-coloured fields running on until they met that sky. The horses worked here in summer; the neighbours passed on their way to town; and over yonder, in the cornfield, Rosicky's own cattle would be eating fodder as winter came on. Nothing could be more undeathlike than this place; nothing could be more right for a man who had helped to do the work of great cities and had always longed for the open country and had got to it at last. Rosicky's life seemed to him complete and beautiful.

THE SKY IS GRAY

Ernest J. Gaines

I

Go'n be coming in a few minutes. Coming 'round that
bend down there full speed. And I'm go'n get out my
hankercher and I'm go'n wave it down, and us go'n get on
it and go.

I keep on looking for it, but Mama don't look that way
no more. She looking down the road where us jest come
from. It's a long old road, and far's you can see you don't
see nothing but gravel. You got dry weeds on both sides, and
you got trees on both sides, and fences on both sides, too.
And you got cows in the pastures and they standing close
together. And when us was coming out yer to catch the bus
I seen the smoke coming out o' the cow's nose.

I look at my mama and I know what she thinking. I been
with Mama so much, jest me and her, I know what she
thinking all the time. Right now it's home — Auntie and
them. She thinking if they got 'nough wood — if she left
'nough there to keep 'em warm till us get back. She thinking
if it go'n rain and if any of 'em go'n have to go out in the
rain. She thinking 'bout the hog — if he go'n get out, and if
Ty and Val be able to get him back in. She always worry like
that when she leave the house. She don't worry too much if
she leave me there with the smaller ones 'cause she know I'm
go'n look after 'em and look after Auntie and everything
else. I'm the oldest and she say I'm the man.

I look at my mama and I love my mama. She wearing that
black coat and that black hat and she looking sad. I love my
mama and I want put my arm 'round her and tell her. But
I'm not s'pose to do that. She say that's weakness and that's

cry-baby stuff, and she don't want no cry-baby 'round her.
She don't want you to be scared neither. 'Cause Ty scared of
ghosts and she always whipping him. I'm scared of the dark,
too. But I make 'tend I ain't. I make 'tend I ain't 'cause I'm
the oldest, and I got to set a good sample for the rest. I can't
ever be scared and I can't ever cry. And that's the reason I
didn't never say nothing 'bout my teef. It been hurting me
and hurting me close to a month now. But I didn't say it. I
didn't say it 'cause I didn't want act like no cry-baby, and
'cause I know us didn't have 'nough money to have it pulled.
But, Lord, it been hurting me. And look like it won't start
till at night when you trying to get little sleep. Then soon's
you shet your eyes — umm-umm, Lord, Look like it go right
down to your heart string.

"Hurting, hanh?" Ty'd say.

I'd shake my head, but I wouldn't open my mouth for
nothing. You open your mouth and let that wind in, and it
almost kill you.

I'd just lay there and listen to 'em snore. Ty, there, right
'side me, and Auntie and Val over by the fireplace. Val
younger 'an me and Ty, and he sleep with Auntie. Mama
sleep 'round the other side with Louis and Walker.

I'd just lay there and listen to 'em, and listen to that wind
out there, and listen to that fire in the fireplace. Sometime
it'd stop long enough to let me get little rest. Sometime it just
hurt, hurt, hurt. Lord, have mercy.

II

Auntie knowed it was hurting me. I didn't tell nobody but
Ty, 'cause us buddies and he ain't go'n tell nobody. But some
kind o' way Auntie found out. When she asked me, I told
her no, nothing was wrong. But she knowed it all the time.
She told me to mash up a piece o' aspirin and wrap it in some
cotton and jugg it down in that hole. I did it, but it didn't
do no good. It stopped for a little while, and started right

back again. She wanted to tell Mama, but I told her Uh-uh.
'Cause I knowed it didn't have no money, and it jest was
go'n make her mad again. So she told Monsieur Bayonne,
and Monsieur Bayonne came to the house and told me to
kneel down 'side him on the fireplace. He put his finger in
his mouth and made the Sign of the Cross on my jaw. The
tip of Monsieur Bayonne finger is some hard, 'cause he
always playing on that guitar. If us sit outside at night us can
always hear Monsieur Bayonne playing on his guitar.
Sometime us leave him out there playing on the guitar.

He made the Sign of the Cross over and over on my jaw,
but that didn't do no good. Even when he prayed and told
me to pray some, too, that teef still hurt.

"How you feeling?" he say.

"Same," I say.

He kept on praying and making the Sign of the Cross and
I kept on praying, too.

"Still hurting?" he say.

"Yes, sir."

Monsieur Bayonne mashed harder and harder on my jaw.
He mashed so hard he almost pushed me on Ty. But then he
stopped.

"What kind o' prayers you praying, boy?" he say.

"Baptist," I say.

"Well, I'll be — no wonder that teef still killing him. I'm
going one way and he going the other. Boy, don't you know
any Catholic prayers?"

"Hail Mary," I say.

"Then you better start saying it."

"Yes, sir."

He started mashing again, and I could hear him praying at
the same time. And, sure 'nough, afterwhile it stopped.

Me and Ty went outside where Monsieur Bayonne two
hounds was, and us started playing with 'em. "Let's go
hunting," Ty say. "All right," I say; and us went on back in

the pasture. Soon the hounds got on a trail, and me and
Ty followed 'em all cross the pasture and then back in
the woods, too. And then they cornered this little old rabbit
and killed him, and me and Ty made 'em get back, and us
picked up the rabbit and started on back home. But it had
started hurting me again. It was hurting me plenty now,
but I wouldn't tell Monsieur Bayonne. That night I didn't
sleep a bit, and first thing in the morning Auntie told me
go back and let Monsieur Bayonne pray over me some
more. Monsieur Bayonne was in his kitchen making coffee
when I got there. Soon's he seen me, he knowed what was
wrong.

"All right, kneel down there 'side that stove," he say. "And
this time pray Catholic. I don't know nothing 'bout Baptist,
and don't want know nothing 'bout him."

III

Last night Mama say: "Tomorrow us going to town."

"It ain't hurting me no more," I say. "I can eat anything
on it."

"Tomorrow us going to town," she say.

And after she finished eating, she got up and went to bed.
She always go to bed early now. 'Fore Daddy went in the
Army, she used to stay up late. All o' us sitting out on the
gallery or 'round the fire. But now, look like soon's she finish
eating she go to bed.

This morning when I woke up, her and Auntie was
standing 'fore the fireplace. She say: "'Nough to get there
and back. Dollar and a half to have it pulled. Twenty-five for
me to go, twenty-five for him. Twenty-five for me to come
back, twenty-five for him. Fifty cents left. Guess I get a little
piece o' salt meat with that."

"Sure can use a piece," Auntie say. "White beans and no
salt meat ain't white beans."

"I do the best I can," Mama say.

They was quiet after that, and I made 'tend I was still sleep.

"James, hit the floor," Auntie say.

I still made 'tend I was sleep. I didn't want 'em to know I was listening.

"All right," Auntie say, shaking me by the shoulder. "Come on. Today's the day."

I pushed the cover down to get out, and Ty grabbed it and pulled it back.

"You, too, Ty," Auntie say.

"I ain't getting no teef pulled," Ty say.

"Don't mean it ain't time to get up," Auntie say. "Hit it, Ty."

Ty got up grumbling.

"James, you hurry up and get in your clothes and eat your food," Auntie say. "What time y'all coming back?" she say to Mama.

"That 'leven o'clock bus," Mama say. "Got to get back in that field this evening."

"Get a move on you, James," Auntie say.

I went in the kitchen and washed my face, then I ate my breakfast. I was having bread and syrup. The bread was warm and hard and tasted good. And I tried to make it last a long time.

Ty came back there, grumbling and mad at me.

"Got to get up," he say. "I ain't having no teef pulled. What I got to be getting up for."

Ty poured some syrup in his pan and got a piece of bread. He didn't wash his hands, neither his face, and I could see that white stuff in his eyes.

"You the one getting a teef pulled," he say. "What I got to get up for. I bet you if I was getting a teef pulled, you wouldn't be getting up. Shucks; syrup again. I'm getting tired of this old syrup. Syrup, syrup, syrup. I want me some bacon sometime."

"Go out in the field and work and you can have bacon,"

Auntie say. She stood in the middle door looking at Ty. "You
better be glad you got syrup. Some people ain't got that —
hard's time is."

"Shucks," Ty say. "How can I be strong."

"I don't know too much 'bout your strength," Auntie say;
"but I know where you go'n be hot, you keep that grumbling
up. James, get a move on you; your mama waiting."

I ate my last piece of bread and went in the front room.
Mama was standing 'fore the fireplace warming her hands. I
put on my coat and my cap, and us left the house.

IV

I look down there again, but it still ain't coming. I almost
say, "It ain't coming, yet," but I keep my mouth shet. 'Cause
that's something else she don't like. She don't like for you to
say something just for nothing. She can see it ain't coming,
I can see it ain't coming, so why say it ain't coming. I don't
say it, and I turn and look at the river that's back o' us. It
so cold the smoke just raising up from the water. I see a
bunch of pull-doos not too far out — jest on the other side
the lilies. I'm wondering if you can eat pull-doos. I ain't too
sure, 'cause I ain't never ate none. But I done ate owls and
black birds, and I done ate red birds, too. I didn't want kill
the red birds, but she made me kill 'em. They had two of 'em
back there. One in my trap, one in Ty trap. Me and Ty was
go'n play with 'em and let 'em go. But she made me kill 'em
'cause us needed the food.

"I can't," I say. "I can't."

"Here," she say. "Take it."

"I can't," I say. "I can't. I can't kill him, Mama. Please."

"Here," she say. "Take this fork, James."

"Please, Mama, I can't kill him," I say.

I could tell she was go'n hit me. And I jecked back, but I
didn't jeck back soon enough.

"Take it," she say.

I took it and reached in for him, but he kept hopping to the back.

"I can't, Mama," I say. The water just kept running down my face. "I can't."

"Get him out o' there," she say.

I reached in for him and he kept hopping to the back. Then I reached in farther, and he pecked me on the hand.

"I can't, Mama," I say.

She slapped me again.

I reached in again, but he kept hopping out my way. Then he hopped to one side, and I reached there. The fork got him on the leg and I heard his leg pop. I pulled my hand out 'cause I had hurt him.

"Give it here," she say, and jecked the fork out my hand.

She reached and got the little bird right in the neck. I heard the fork go in his neck, and I heard it go in the ground. She brought him out and helt him right in front o' me.

"That's one," she say. She shook him off and gived me the fork. "Get the other one."

"I can't, Mama. I do anything. But I can't do that."

She went to the corner o' the fence and broke the biggest switch over there. I knelt 'side the trap crying.

"Get him out o' there," she say.

"I can't, Mama."

She started hitting me cross the back. I went down on the ground crying.

"Get him," she say.

"Octavia," Auntie say.

'Cause she had come out o' the house and she was standing by the tree looking at us.

"Get him out o' there," Mama say.

"Octavia," Auntie say; "explain to him. Explain to him. Jest don't beat him. Explain to him."

But she hit me and hit me and hit me.

I'm still young. I ain't no more'an eight. But I know now.

I know why I had to. (They was so little, though. They was so little. I 'member how I picked the feathers off 'em and cleaned 'em and helt 'em over the fire. Then us all ate 'em. Ain't had but little bitty piece, but us all had little bitty piece, and ever'body jest looked at me, 'cause they was so proud.) S'pose she had to go away? That's why I had to do it. S'pose she had to go away like Daddy went away? Then who was go'n look after us? They had to be somebody left to carry on. I didn't know it then, but I know it now. Auntie and Monsieur Bayonne talked to me and made me see.

V

Time I see it, I get out my hankercher and start waving. It still 'way down there, but I keep waving anyhow. Then it come closer and stop and me and Mama get on. Mama tell me go sit in the back while she pay. I do like she say, and the people look at me. When I pass the little sign that say White and Colored, I start looking for a seat. I jest see one of 'em back there, but I don't take it, 'cause I want my mama to sit down herself. She come in the back and sit down, and I lean on the seat. They got seats in the front, but I know I can't sit there, 'cause I have to sit back o' the sign. Anyhow, I don't want sit there if my mama go'n sit back here.

They got a lady sitting 'side my mama and she look at me and grin little bit. I grin back, but I don't open my mouth, 'cause the wind'll get in and make that teef hurt. The lady take out a pack o' gum and reach me a slice, but I shake my head. She reach Mama a slice, and Mama shake her head. The lady jest can't understand why a little boy'll turn down gum, and she reached me a slice again. This time I point to my jaw. The lady understand and grin little bit, and I grin little bit, but I don't open my mouth, though.

They got a girl sitting 'cross from me. She got on a red overcoat, and her hair plaited in one big plait. First, I make 'tend I don't even see her. But then I start looking at her little bit. She make 'tend she don't see me neither, but I catch her looking that way. She got a cold, and ever' now and then she hist that little hankercher to her nose. She ought to blow it, but she don't. Must think she too much a lady or something.

Ever' time she hist that little hankercher, the lady 'side her say something in her yer. She shake her head and lay her hands in her lap again. Then I catch her kind o' looking where I'm at. I grin at her. But think she'll grin back? No. She turn up her little old nose like I got some snot on my face or something. Well, I show her both o' us can turn us head. I turn mine, too, and look out at the river.

The river is gray. The sky is gray. They have pull-doos on the water. The water is wavey, and the pull-doos go up and down. The bus go 'round a turn, and you got plenty trees hiding the river. Then the bus go 'round another turn, and I can see the river again.

I look to the front where all the white people sitting. Then I look at that little old gal again. I don't look right at her, 'cause I don't want all them people to know I love her. I jest look at her little bit, like I'm looking out that window over there. But she know I'm looking that way, and she kind o' look at me, too. The lady sitting 'side her catch her this time, and she lean over and say something in her yer.

"I don't love him nothing," that little old gal say out loud.

Ever'body back there yer her mouth, and all of 'em look at us and laugh.

"I don't love you, neither," I say. "So you don't have to turn up your nose, Miss."

"You the one looking," she say.

"I wasn't looking at you," I say. "I was looking out that window, there."

"Out that window, my foot," she say. "I seen you. Ever' time I turn 'round you look at me."

"You must o' been looking yourself if you seen me all them times," I say.

"Shucks," she say. "I got me all kind o' boyfriends."

"I got girlfriends, too," I say.

"Well, I just don't want you to get your hopes up," she say. I don't say no more to that little old gal, 'cause I don't want have to bust her in the mouth. I lean on the seat where Mama sitting, and I don't even look that way no more. When us get to Bayonne, she jugg her little old tongue out at me. I make 'tend I'm go'n hit her, and she duck down side her mama. And all the people laugh at us again.

VI

Me and Mama get off and start walking in town. Bayonne is a little bitty town. Baton Rouge is a hundred times bigger 'an Bayonne. I went to Baton Rouge once — me, Ty, Mama, and Daddy. But that was 'way back yonder — 'fore he went in the Army. I wonder when us go'n see him again. I wonder when. Look like he ain't ever coming home. . . . Even the pavement all cracked in Bayonne. Got grass shooting right out the sidewalk. Got weeds in the ditch, too; jest like they got home.

It some cold in Bayonne. Look like it colder 'an it is home. The wind blow in my face, and I feel that stuff running down my nose. I sniff. Mama say use that hankercher. I blow my nose and put it back.

Us pass a school and I see them white children playing in the yard. Big old red school, and them children jest running and playing. Then us pass a café, and I see a bunch of 'em in there eating. I wish I was in there 'cause I'm cold. Mama tell me keep my eyes in front where they blonks.

Us pass stores that got dummies, and us pass another café, and then us pass a shoe shop, and that baldhead man in there fixing on a shoe. I look at him and I butt into that white lady, and Mama jeck me in front and tell me stay there.

Us come to the courthouse, and I see the flag waving there. This one yer ain't like the one us got at school. This one yer

ain't got but a handful of stars. One at school got a big pile
of stars — one for ever' state. Us pass it and us turn and
there it is — the dentist office. Me and Mama go in, and they
got people sitting ever' where you look. They even got a little
boy in there younger 'an me.

Me and Mama sit on that bench, and a white lady come
in there and ask me what my name. Mama tell her, and the
white lady go back. Then I yer somebody hollering in there.
And soon's that little boy hear him hollering, he start
hollering, too. His mama pat him and pat him, trying to
make him hush up, but he ain't thinking 'bout her.

The man that was hollering in there come out holding his
jaw.

"Got it, hanh?" another man say.

The man shake his head.

"Man, I thought they was killing you in there," the other
man say. "Hollering like a pig under a gate."

The man don't say nothing. He jest head for the door, and
the other man follow him.

"John Lee," the white lady say. "John Lee Williams."

The little boy jugg his head down in his mama lap and
holler more now. His mama tell him go with the nurse, but
he ain't thinking 'bout her. His mama tell him again, but he
don't even yer. His mama pick him up and take him in there,
and even when the white lady shet the door I can still hear
him hollering.

"I often wonder why the Lord let a child like that suffer,"
a lady say to my mama. The lady's sitting right in front o'
us on another bench. She got on a white dress and a black
sweater. She must be a nurse or something herself, I reckoned.

"Not us to question," a man say.

"Sometimes I don't know if we shouldn't," the lady say.

"I know definitely we shouldn't," the man say. The man
look like a preacher. He big and fat and he got on a black

suit. He got a gold chain, too.

"Why?" the lady say.

"Why anything?" the preacher say.

"Yes," the lady say. "Why anything?"

"Not us to question," the preacher say.

The lady look at the preacher a little while and look at Mama again.

"And look like it's the poor who do most the suffering," she say. "I don't understand it."

"Best not to even try," the preacher say. "He works in mysterious ways. Wonders to perform."

Right then Little John Lee bust out hollering, and ever'body turn they head.

"He's not a good dentist," the lady say. "Dr. Robillard is much better. But more expensive. That's why most of the colored people come here. The white people go to Dr. Robillard. Y'all from Bayonne?"

"Down the river," my mama say. And that's all she go'n say, 'cause she don't talk much. But the lady keep on looking at her, and so she say: "Near Morgan."

"I see," the lady say.

VII

"That's the trouble with the black people in this country today," somebody else say. This one yer sitting on the same side me and Mama sitting, and he kind o' sitting in front of that preacher. He look like a teacher or somebody that go to college. He got on a suit, and he got a book that he been reading. "We don't question is exactly the trouble," he say. "We should question and question and question. Question everything."

The preacher jest look at him a long time. He done put a toothpick or something in his mouth, and he jest keep turning it and turning it. You can see he don't like that boy with that book.

"Maybe you can explain what you mean," he say.

"I said what I meant," the boy say. "Question everything. Every stripe, every star, every word spoken. Everything."

"It 'pears to me this young lady and I was talking 'bout God, young man," the preacher say.

"Question Him, too," the boy say.

"Wait," the preacher say. "Wait now."

"You heard me right," the boy say. "His existence as well as everything else. Everything."

The preacher jest look cross the room at the boy. You can see he getting madder and madder. But mad or no mad, the boy ain't thinking 'bout him. He look at the preacher jest's hard's the preacher look at him.

"Is this what they coming to?" the preacher say. "Is this what we educating them for?"

"You're not educating me," the boy say. "I wash dishes at night to go to school in the day. So even the words you spoke need questioning."

The preacher jest look at him and shake his head.

"When I come in this room and seen you there with your book, I said to myself, There's an intelligent man. How wrong a person can be."

"Show me one reason to believe in the existence of a God," the boy say.

"My heart tell me," the preacher say.

"My heart tells me," the boy say. "My heart tells me. Sure, my heart tells me. And as long as you listen to what your heart tells you, you will have only what the white man gives you and nothing more. Me, I don't listen to my heart. The purpose of the heart is to pump blood throughout the body, and nothing else."

"Who's your paw, boy?" the preacher say.

"Why?"

"Who is he?"

"He's dead."

"And your mom?"

"She's in Charity Hospital with pneumonia. Half killed herself working for nothing."

"And 'cause he's dead and she sick, you mad at the world?"

"I'm not mad at the world. I'm questioning the world. I'm questioning it with cold logic, sir. What do words like Freedom, Liberty, God, White, Colored mean? I want to know. That's why *you* are sending us to school, to read and to ask questions. And because we ask these questions, you call us mad. No, sir, it is not us who are mad."

"You keep saying 'us'?"

"'Us' . . . why not? I'm not alone."

The preacher jest shake his head. Then he look at ever'body in the room — ever'body. Some of the people look down at the floor, keep from looking at him. I kind o' look 'way myself, but soon's I know he done turn his head, I look that way again.

"I'm sorry for you," he say.

"Why?" the boy say. "Why not be sorry for yourself? Why are you so much better off than I am? Why aren't you sorry for these other people in here? Why not be sorry for the lady who had to drag her child into the dentist office? Why not be sorry for the lady sitting on that bench over there? Be sorry for them. Not for me. Some way or other I'm going to make it."

"No, I'm sorry for you," the preacher say.

"Of course. Of course," the boy say, shaking his head. "You're sorry for me because I rock that pillar you're leaning on."

"You can't ever rock the pillar I'm leaning on, young man. It's stronger than anything man can ever do."

"You believe in God because a man told you to believe in God. A white man told you to believe in God. And why? To keep you ignorant, so he can keep you under his feet."

"So now, we the ignorant?"

"Yes," the boy say. "Yes." And he open his book again.

The preacher jest look at him there. The boy done forgot all about him. Ever'body else make 'tend they done forgot 'bout the squabble, too.

Then I see that preacher getting up real slow. Preacher a great big old man, and he got to brace hisself to get up. He come 'cross the room where the boy is. He jest stand there looking at him, but the boy don't raise his head.

"Stand up, boy," preacher say.

The boy look up at him, then he shet his book real slow and stand up. Preacher jest draw back and hit him in the face. The boy fall 'gainst the wall, but he straighten hisself up and look right back at that preacher.

"You forgot the other cheek," he say.

The preacher hit him again on the other side. But this time the boy don't fall.

"That hasn't changed a thing," he say.

The preacher jest look at the boy. The preacher breathing real hard like he jest run up a hill. The boy sit down and open his book again.

"I feel sorry for you," the preacher say. "I never felt so sorry for a man before."

The boy make 'tend he don't even hear that preacher. He keep on reading his book. The preacher go back and get his hat off the chair.

"Excuse me," he say to us. "I'll come back some other time. Y'all, please excuse me."

And he look at the boy and go out the room. The boy hist his hand up to his mouth one time, to wipe 'way some blood. All the rest o' the time he keep on reading.

VIII

The lady and her little boy come out the dentist, and the nurse call somebody else in. Then little bit later they come out, and the nurse call another name. But fast's she call somebody in there, somebody else come in the place where we at, and the room stay full.

The people coming in now, all of 'em wearing big coats. One of 'em say something 'bout sleeting, and another one say he hope not. Another one say he think it ain't nothing but rain. 'Cause, he say, rain can get awful cold this time o' year.

All 'cross the room they talking. Some of 'em talking to people right by 'em, some of 'em talking to people clare 'cross the room, some of 'em talking to anybody'll listen. It's a little bitty room, no bigger 'an us kitchen, and I can see ever'body in there. The little old room 's full of smoke, 'cause you got two old men smoking pipes. I think I feel my teef thumping me some, and I hold my breath and wait. I wait and wait, but it don't thump me no more. Thank God for that.

I feel like going to sleep, and I lean back 'gainst the wall. But I'm scared to go to sleep: Scared 'cause the nurse might call my name and I won't hear her. And Mama might go to sleep, too, and she be mad if neither us heard the nurse.

I look up at Mama. I love my mama. I love my mama. And when cotton come I'm go'n get her a newer coat. And I ain't go'n get a black one neither. I think I'm go'n get her a red one.

"They got some books over there," I say. "Want read one of 'em?"

Mama look at the books, but she don't answer me.

"You got yourself a little man there," the lady say.

Mama don't say nothing to the lady, but she must 'a' grin a little bit, 'cause I seen the lady grinning back. The lady look at me a little while, like she feeling sorry for me.

"You sure got that preacher out here in a hurry," she say to that other boy.

The boy look up at her and look in his book again. When

I grow up I want be jest like him. I want clothes like that and I want keep a book with me, too.

"You really don't believe in God?" the lady say.

"No," he say.

"But why?" the lady say.

"Because the wind is pink," he say.

"What?" the lady say.

The boy don't answer her no more. He jest read in his book.

"Talking 'bout the wind is pink," that old lady say. She sitting on the same bench with the boy, and she trying to look in his face. The boy make 'tend the old lady ain't even there. He jest keep reading. "Wind is pink," she say again. "Eh, Lord, what children go'n be saying next?"

The lady 'cross from us bust out laughing.

"That's a good one," she say. "The wind is pink. Yes, sir, that's a good one."

"Don't you believe the wind is pink?" the boy say. He keep his head down in the book.

"Course I believe it, Honey," the lady say. "Course I do." She look at us and wink her eye. "And what color is grass, Honey?"

"Grass? Grass is black."

She bust out laughing again. The boy look at her.

"Don't you believe grass is black?" he say.

The lady quit laughing and look at him. Ever'body else look at him now. The place quiet, quiet.

"Grass is green, Honey," the lady say. "It was green yesterday, it's green today, and it's go'n be green tomorrow."

"How do you know it's green?"

"I know because I know."

"You don't know it's green. You believe it's green because someone told you it was green. If someone had told you it was black you'd believe it was black."

"It's green," the lady say. "I know green when I see green."

"Prove it's green."

"Surely, now," the lady say. "Don't tell me it's coming to that?"

"It's coming to just that," the boy say. "Words mean nothing. One means no more than the other."

"That's what it all coming to?" that old lady say. That old lady got on a turban and she got on two sweaters. She got a green sweater under a black sweater. I can see the green sweater 'cause some of the buttons on the other sweater missing.

"Yes, ma'am," the boy say. "Words mean nothing. Action is the only thing. Doing. That's the only thing."

"Other words, you want the Lord to come down here and show Hisself to you?" she say.

"Exactly, ma'am."

"You don't mean that, I'm sure?"

"I do, ma'am."

"Done, Jesus," the old lady say, shaking her head.

"I didn't go 'long with that preacher at first," the other lady say; "but now — I don't know. When a person say the grass is black, he's either a lunatic or something wrong."

"Prove to me that it's green."

"It's green because the people say it's green."

"Those same people say we're citizens of the United States."

"I think I'm a citizen."

"Citizens have certain rights. Name me one right that you have. One right, granted by the Constitution, that you can exercise in Bayonne."

The lady don't answer him. She jest look at him like she don't know what he talking 'bout. I know I don't.

"Things changing," she say.

"Things are changing because some black men have begun to follow their brains instead of their hearts."

"You trying to say these people don't believe in God?"

"I'm sure some of them do. Maybe most of them do. But they don't believe that God is going to touch these white people's hearts and change them tomorrow. Things change through action. By no other way."

Ever'body sit quiet and look at the boy. Nobody say a thing. Then the lady 'cross from me and Mama jest shake her head.

"Let's hope that not all your generation feel the same way you do," she say.

"Think what you please, it doesn't matter," the boy say. "But it will be men who listen to their heads and not their hearts who will see that your children have a better chance than you had."

"Let's hope they ain't all like you, though," the old lady say. "Done forgot the heart absolutely."

"Yes, ma'am, I hope they aren't all like me," the boy say. "Unfortunately I was born too late to believe in your God. Let's hope that the ones who come after will have your faith — if not in your God, then in something else, something definitely that they can lean on. I haven't anything. For me, the wind is pink; the grass is black."

IX

The nurse come in the room where us all sitting and waiting and say the doctor won't take no more patients till one o'clock this evening. My mama jump up off the bench and go up to the white lady.

"Nurse, I have to go back in the field this evening," she say.

"The doctor is treating his last patient now," the nurse say. "One o'clock this evening."

"Can I at least speak to the doctor?" my mama say.

"I'm his nurse," the lady say.

"My little boy sick," my mama say. "Right now his teef almost killing him."

The nurse look at me. She trying to make up her mind if

to let me come in. I look at her real pitiful. The teef ain't
hurting me a tall, but Mama say it is, so I make 'tend for her
sake.

"This evening," the nurse say, and go back in the office.

"Don't feel 'jected, Honey," the lady say to Mama. "I been
'round 'em a long time — they take you when they want to.
If you was white, that's something else; but you the wrong
shade."

Mama don't say nothing to the lady, and me and her go
outside and stand 'gainst the wall. It's cold out there. I can
feel that wind going through my coat. Some of the other
people come out of the room and go up the street. Me and
Mama stand there a little while and start to walking. I don't
know where us going. When us come to the other street us
jest stand there.

"You don't have to make water, do you?" Mama say.

"No, ma'am," I say.

Us go up the street. Walking real slow. I can tell Mama
don't know where she going. When us come to a store us
stand there and look at the dummies. I look at a little boy
with a brown overcoat. He got on brown shoes, too. I look
at my old shoes and look at his'n again. You wait till
summer, I say.

Me and Mama walk away. Us come up to another store
and us stop and look at them dummies, too. Then us go
again. Us pass a café where the white people in there eating.
Mama tell me keep my eyes in front where they blonks, but
I can't help from seeing them people eat. My stomach start
to growling 'cause I'm hungry. When I see people eating, I
get hungry; when I see a coat, I get cold.

A man whistle at my mama when us go by a filling station.
She make 'tend she don't even see him. I look back and I feel
like hitting him in the mouth. If I was bigger, I say. If I was
bigger, you see.

Us keep on going. I'm getting colder and colder, but I don't say nothing. I feel that stuff running down my nose and I sniff.

"That rag," she say.

I git it out and wipe my nose. I'm getting cold all over now — my face, my hands, my feet, ever'thing. Us pass another little café, but this'n for white people, too, and us can't go in there neither. So us jest walk. I'm so cold now, I'm 'bout ready to say it. If I knowed where us was going, I wouldn't be so cold, but I don't know where us going. Us go, us go, us go. Us walk clean out o' Bayonne. Then us cross the street and us come back. Same thing I seen when I got off the bus. Same old trees, same old walk, same old weeds, same old cracked pave — same old ever'thing.

I sniff again.

"That rag," she say.

I wipe my nose real fast and jugg that hankercher back in my pocket 'fore my hand get too cold. I raise my head and I can see David hardware store. When us come up to it, us go in. I don't know why, but I'm glad.

It warm in there. It so warm in there you don't want ever leave. I look for the heater, and I see it over by them ba'ls. Three white men standing 'round the heater talking in Creole. One of 'em come to see what Mama want.

"Got any ax handle?" she say.

Me, Mama, and the white man start to the back, but Mama stop me when us come to the heater. Her and the white man go on. I hold my hand over the heater and look at 'em. They go all the way in the back, and I see the white man point to the ax handle 'gainst the wall. Mama take one of 'em and shake it like she trying to figure how much it weigh. Then she rub her hand over it from one end to the other end. She turn it over and look at the other side, then she shake it again, and shake her head and put it back. She get another one and she do it jest like she did the first one, then she shake her head. Then she get a brown one and do

it that, too. But she don't like this one neither. Then she get
another one, but 'fore she shake it or anything, she look at
me. Look like she trying to say something to me, but I don't
know what it is. All I know is I done got warm now and I'm
feeling right smart better. Mama shake this ax handle jest
like she done the others, and shake her head and say
something to the white man. The white man jest look at his
pile of ax handle, and when Mama pass by him to come to
the front, the white man jest scratch his head and follow her.
She tell me come on, and us go on out and start walking
again.

Us walk and walk, and no time at all I'm cold again. Look
like I'm colder now 'cause I can still remember how good it
was back there. My stomach growl and I suck it in to keep
Mama from yering it. She walking right 'side me, and it
growl so loud you can yer it a mile. But Mama don't say a
word.

X

When us come up to the courthouse, I look at the clock.
It got quarter to twelve. Mean us got another hour and a
quarter to be out yer in the cold. Us go and stand side a
building. Something hit my cap and I look up at the sky. Sleet
falling.

I look at Mama standing there. I want stand close 'side
her, but she don't like that. She say that's cry-baby stuff. She
say you got to stand for yourself, by yourself.

"Let's go back to that office," she say.

Us cross the street. When us get to the dentist I try to open
the door, but I can't. Mama push me on the side and she
twist the knob. But she can't open it neither. She twist it
some more, harder, but she can't open it. She turn 'way from
the door. I look at her, but I don't move and I don't say
nothing. I done seen her like this before and I'm scared.

"You hungry?" she say. She say it like she mad at me, like
I'm the one cause of ever'thing.

"No, ma'am," I say.

"You want eat and walk back, or you rather don't eat and ride?"

"I ain't hungry," I say.

I ain't jest hungry, but I'm cold, too. I'm so hungry and I'm so cold I want cry. And look like I'm getting colder and colder. My feet done got numb. I try to work my toes, but I can't. Look like I'm go'n die. Look like I'm go'n stand right here and freeze to death. I think about home. I think about Val and Auntie and Ty and Louis and Walker. It 'bout twelve o'clock and I know they eating dinner. I can hear Ty making jokes. That's Ty. Always trying to make some kind o' joke. I wish I was right there listening to him. Give anything in the world if I was home 'round the fire.

"Come on," Mama say.

Us start walking again. My feet so numb I can't hardly feel 'em. Us turn the corner and go back up the street. The clock start hitting for twelve.

The sleet's coming down plenty now. They hit the pave and bounce like rice. Oh, Lord; oh, Lord, I pray. Don't let me die. Don't let me die. Don't let me die, Lord.

XI

Now I know where us going. Us going back o' town where the colored people eat. I don't care if I don't eat. I been hungry before. I can stand it. But I can't stand the cold.

I can see us go'n have a long walk. It 'bout a mile down there. But I don't mind. I know when I get there I'm go'n warm myself. I think I can hold out. My hands numb in my pockets and my feet numb, too, but if I keep moving I can hold out. Jest don't stop no more, that's all.

The sky's gray. The sleet keep falling. Falling like rain now — plenty, plenty. You can hear it hitting the pave. You can see it bouncing. Sometime it bounce two times 'fore it settle.

Us keep going. Us don't say nothing. Us jest keep going, keep going.

I wonder what Mama thinking. I hope she ain't mad with me. When summer come I'm go'n pick plenty cotton and get her a coat. I'm go'n get her a red one.

I hope they make it summer all the time. I be glad if it was summer all the time — but it ain't. Us got to have winter, too. Lord, I hate the winter. I guess ever'body hate the winter.

I don't sniff this time. I get out my hankercher and wipe my nose. My hand so cold I can hardly hold the hankercher.

I think us getting close, but us ain't there yet. I wonder where ever'body is. Can't see nobody but us. Look like us the only two people moving 'round today. Must be too cold for the rest of the people to move 'round.

I can hear my teefes. I hope they don't knock together too hard and make that bad one hurt. Lord, that's all I need, for that bad one to start off.

I hear a church bell somewhere. But today ain't Sunday. They must be ringing for a funeral or something.

I wonder what they doing at home. They must be eating. Monsieur Bayonne might be there with his guitar. One day Ty played with Monsieur Bayonne guitar and broke one o' the string. Monsieur Bayonne got some mad with Ty. He say Ty ain't go'n never 'mount to nothing. Ty can go jest like him when he ain't there. Ty can make ever'body laugh mocking Monsieur Bayonne.

I used to like to be with Mama and Daddy. Us used to be happy. But they took him in the Army. Now, nobody happy no more. . . . I be glad when he come back.

Monsieur Bayonne say it wasn't fair for 'em to take Daddy and give Mama nothing and give us nothing. Auntie say, Shhh, Etienne. Don't let 'em yer you talk like that. Monsieur Bayonne say, It's God truth. What they giving his children? They have to walk three and a half mile to school hot or cold. That's anything to give for a paw? She got to work in

the field rain or shine jest to make ends meet. That's anything
to give for a husband? Auntie say, Shhh, Etienne, shhh. Yes,
you right, Monsieur Bayonne say. Best don't say it in front
of 'em now. But one day they go'n find out. One day. Yes,
s'pose so, Auntie say. Then what, Rose Mary? Monsieur
Bayonne say. I don't know, Etienne, Auntie say. All us can
do is us job, and leave ever'thing else in His hand. . . .

Us getting closer, now. Us getting closer. I can see the
railroad tracks.

Us cross the tracks, and now I see the café. Jest to get in
there, I say. Jest to get in there. Already I'm starting to feel
little better.

XII

Us go in. Ahh, it good. I look for the heater; there 'gainst
the wall. One of them little brown ones. I jest stand there
and hold my hand over it. I can't open my hands too wide
'cause they almost froze.

Mama standing right 'side me. She done unbuttoned her
coat. Smoke rise out the coat, and the coat smell like a wet
dog.

I move to the side so Mama can have more room. She open
out her hands and rub 'em together. I rub mine together, too,
'cause this keep 'em from hurting. If you let 'em warm too
fast, they hurt you sure. But if you let 'em warm jest little bit
at a time, and you keep rubbing 'em, they be all right ever'
time.

They got jest two more people in the café. A lady back o'
the counter, and a man on this side the counter. They had
been watching us ever since us come in.

Mama get out the hankercher and count the money. Both
o' us know how much money she got there. Three dollars.
No, she ain't got three dollars. 'Cause she had to pay us way
up here. She ain't got but two dollars and a half left. Dollar
and a half to get my teef pulled, and fifty cents for us to go

back on, and fifty cents worse o' salt meat.

She stir the money 'round with her finger. Most o' the money is change 'cause I can hear it rubbing together. She stir it and stir it. Then she look at the door. It still sleeting. I can yer it hitting 'gainst the wall like rice.

"I ain't hungry, Mama," I say.

"Got to pay 'em something for they heat," she say.

She take a quarter out the hankercher and tie the hankercher up again. She look over her shoulder at the people, but she still don't move. I hope she don't spend the money. I don't want her spend it on me. I'm hungry, I'm almost starving I'm so hungry, but I don't want her spending the money on me.

She flip the quarter over like she thinking. She must be thinking 'bout us walking back home. Lord, I sure don't want walk home. If I thought it done any good to say something, I say it. But my mama make up her own mind.

She turn way from the heater right fast, like she better hurry up and do it 'fore she change her mind. I turn to look at her go to the counter. The man and the lady look at her, too. She tell the lady something and the lady walk away. The man keep on looking at her. Her back turn to the man, and Mama don't even know he standing there.

The lady put some cakes and a glass o' milk on the counter. Then she pour up a cup o' coffee and set it side the other stuff. Mama pay her for the things and come back where I'm at. She tell me sit down at that table 'gainst the wall.

The milk and the cakes for me. The coffee for my mama. I eat slow, and I look at her. She looking outside at the sleet. She looking real sad. I say to myself, I'm go'n make all this up one day. You see, one day, I'm go'n make all this up. I want to say it now. I want to tell how I feel right now. But Mama don't like for us to talk like that.

"I can't eat all this," I say.

They got just three little cakes there. And I'm so hungry

right now, the Lord know I can eat a hundred times three. But I want her to have one.

She don't even look my way. She know I'm hungry. She know I want it. I let it stay there a while, then I get it and eat it. I eat jest on my front teefes, 'cause if it tech that back teef I know what'll happen. Thank God it ain't hurt me a tall today.

After I finish eating I see the man go to the juke box. He drop a nickel in it, then he jest stand there looking at the record. Mama tell me keep my eyes in front where they blonks. I turn my head like she say, but then I yer the man coming towards us.

"Dance, Pretty?" he say.

Mama get up to dance with him. But 'fore you know it, she done grabbed the little man and done throwed him 'side the wall. He hit the wall so hard he stop the juke box from playing.

The little man jump up off the floor and start towards my mama. 'Fore you know it, Mama done sprung open her knife and she waiting for him.

"Come on," she say. "Come on. I'll cut you from your neighbo to your throat. Come on."

I go up to the little man to hit him, but Mama make me come and stand 'side her. The little man look at me and Mama and go back to the counter.

XIII

"Fasten that coat. Let's go," Mama say.

"You don't have to leave," the lady say.

Mama don't answer the lady, and us right out in the cold again. I'm warm right now — my hands, my yers, my feet — but I know this ain't go'n last too long. It done sleet so much now you got ice ever'where.

Us cross the railroad tracks, and soon's us do, I get cold. That wind go through this little old coat like it ain't nothing.

I got a shirt and a sweater under it, but that wind don't pay 'em no mind. I look up and I can see us got a long way to go. I wonder if us go'n make it 'fore I get too cold.

Us cross over to walk on the sidewalk. They got jest one sidewalk back here. It's over there.

After us go jest a little piece, I smell bread cooking. I look, then I see a baker shop. When us get closer, I can smell it more better. I shet my eyes and make 'tend I'm eating. But I keep 'em shet too long and I butt up 'gainst a telephone post. Mama grab me and see if I'm hurt. I ain't bleeding or nothing and she turn me loose.

I can feel I'm getting colder and colder, and I look up to see how far us still got to go. Uptown is 'way up yonder. A half mile, I reckoned. I try to think of something. They say think and you won't get cold. I think of that poem, *Annabel Lee*. I ain't been to school in so long — this bad weather — I reckoned they done passed *Annabel Lee*. But passed it or not, I'm sure Miss Walker go'n make me recite it when I get there. That woman don't never forget nothing. I ain't never seen nobody like that.

I'm still getting cold. *Annabel Lee* or no *Annabel Lee*, I'm still getting cold. But I can see us getting closer. Us getting there gradually.

Soon's us turn the corner, I see a little old white lady up in front o' us. She the only lady on the street. She all in black and she got a long black rag over her head.

"Stop," she say.

Me and Mama stop and look at her. She must be crazy to be out in all this sleet. Ain't got but a few other people out there, and all of 'em men.

"Yall done ate?" she say.

"Jest finished," Mama say.

"Yall must be cold then?" she say.

"Us headed for the dentist," Mama say. "Us'll warm up when us get there."

"What dentist?" the old lady say. "Mr. Bassett?"

"Yes, ma'am," Mama say.

"Come on in," the old lady say. "I'll telephone him and tell him yall coming."

Me and Mama follow the old lady in the store. It's a little bitty store, and it don't have much in there. The old lady take off her head piece and fold it up.

"Helena?" somebody call from the back.

"Yes, Alnest?" the old lady say.

"Did you see them?"

"They're here. Standing beside me."

"Good. Now you can stay inside."

The old lady look at Mama. Mama waiting to hear what she brought us in here for. I'm waiting for that, too.

"I saw yall each time you went by," she say. "I came out to catch you, but you were gone."

"Us went back o' town," Mama say.

"Did you eat?"

"Yes, ma'am."

The old lady look at Mama a long time, like she thinking Mama might be jest saying that. Mama look right back at her. The old lady look at me to see what I got to say. I don't say nothing. I sure ain't going 'gainst my mama.

"There's food in the kitchen," she say to Mama. "I've been keeping it warm."

Mama turn right around and start for the door.

"Just a minute," the old lady say. Mama stop. "The boy'll have to work for it. It isn't free."

"Us don't take no handout," Mama say.

"I'm not handing out anything," the old lady say. "I need my garbage moved to the front. Ernest has a bad cold and can't go out there."

"James'll move it for you," Mama say.

"Not unless you eat," the old lady say. "I'm old, but I have my pride, too, you know."

Mama can see she ain't go'n beat this old lady down, so she jest shake her head.

"All right," the old lady say. "Come into the kitchen."

She lead the way with that rag in her hand. The kitchen is a little bitty little thing, too. The table and the stove jest about fill it up. They got a little room to the side. Somebody in there laying cross the bed. Must be the person she was talking with: Alnest or Ernest — I forget what she call him.

"Sit down," the old lady say to Mama. "Not you," she say to me. "You have to move the cans."

"Helena?" somebody say in the other room.

"Yes, Alnest?" the old lady say.

"Are you going out there again?"

"I must show the boy where the garbage is," the old lady say.

"Keep that shawl over your head," the old man say.

"You don't have to remind me. Come, boy," the old lady say.

Us go out in the yard. Little old back yard ain't no bigger 'an the store or the kitchen. But it can sleet here jest like it can sleet in any big back yard. And 'fore you know it I'm trembling.

"There," the old lady say, pointing to the cans. I pick up one of the cans. The can so light I put it back down to look inside o' it.

"Here," the old lady say. "Leave that cap alone."

I look at her in the door. She got that black rag wrapped 'round her shoulders, and she pointing one of her fingers at me.

"Pick it up and carry it to the front," she say. I go by her with the can. I'm sure the thing 's empty. She could 'a' carried the thing by herself, I'm sure. "Set it on the sidewalk by the door and come back for the other one," she say.

I go and come back, Mama look at me when I pass her. I get the other can and take it to the front. It don't feel no heavier 'an the other one. I tell myself to look inside and see just what I been hauling. First, I look up and down the street. Nobody coming. Then I look over my shoulder. Little old lady done slipped there jest 's quiet 's mouse, watching me. Look like she knowed I was go'n try that.

"Ehh, Lord," she say. "Children, children. Come in here, boy, and go wash your hands."

I follow her into the kitchen, and she point, and I go to the bathroom. When I come out, the old lady done dished up the food. Rice, gravy, meat, and she even got some lettuce and tomato in a saucer. She even got a glass o' milk and a piece o' cake there, too. It look so good. I almost start eating 'fore I say my blessing.

"Helena?" the old man say.

"Yes, Ernest?" she say.

"Are they eating?"

"Yes," she say.

"Good," he say. "Now you'll stay inside."

The old lady go in there where he is and I can hear 'em talking. I look at Mama. She eating slow like she thinking. I wonder what 's the matter now. I reckoned she think 'bout home.

The old lady come back in the kitchen.

"I talked to Dr. Bassett's nurse," she say. "Dr. Bassett will take you as soon as you get there."

"Thank you, ma'am," Mama say.

"Perfectly all right," the old lady say. "Which one is it?"

Mama nod towards me. The old lady look at me real sad. I look sad, too.

"You're not afraid, are you?" she say.

"No'm," I say.

"That's a good boy," the old lady say. "Nothing to be afraid of."

When me and Mama get through eating, us thank the old lady again.

"Helena, are they leaving?" the old man say.

"Yes, Alnest."

"Tell them I say good-by."

"They can hear you, Ernest."

"Good-by both mother and son," the old man say. "And may God be with you."

Me and Mama tell the old man good-by, and us follow the old lady in the front. Mama open the door to go out, but she stop and come back in the store.

"You sell salt meat?" she say.

"Yes."

"Give me two bits worse."

"That isn't very much salt meat," the old lady say.

"That's all I have," Mama say.

The old lady go back o' the counter and cut a big piece off the chunk. Then she wrap it and put it in a paper bag.

"Two bits," she say.

"That look like awful lot of meat for a quarter," Mama say.

"Two bits," the old lady say. "I've been selling salt meat behind this counter twenty-five years. I think I know what I'm doing."

"You got a scale there," Mama say.

"What?" the old lady say.

"Weigh it," Mama say.

"What?" the old lady say. "Are you telling me how to run my business?"

"Thanks very much for the food," Mama say.

"Just a minute," the old lady say.

"James," Mama say to me. I move towards the door.

"Just one minute, I said," the old lady say.

Me and Mama stop again and look at her. The old lady take the meat out the bag and unwrap it and cut 'bout half o' it off. Then she wrap it up again and jugg it back in the bag and give it to Mama. Mama lay the quarter on the counter.

"Your kindness will never be forgotten," she say. "James," she say to me.

Us go out, and the old lady come to the door to look at us. After us go a little piece I look back, and she still there watching us.

The sleet 's coming down heavy, heavy now, and I turn up my collar to keep my neck warm. My mama tell me turn it right back down.

"You not a bum," she say. "You a man."